Snow Plain

Duo Duo

Translated by
John A. Crespi

with contributions from
Harriet Evans, Jiang Hong,
Gregory B. Lee, Larry McCaffery,
and Danny Wang

ZEPHYR PRESS

The stories "Going Home" and "Vacation" appeared in earlier versions in *Abandoned Wine* (WellSweep Press, 1996), and "The Day I Got to Xi'an" in the anthology *Chairman Mao Would Not Be Amused* (Grove Press, 1995).

Zephyr Press acknowledges with gratitude the financial support of The National Endowment for the Arts and the Massachusetts Cultural Council.

massculturalcouncil.org

NATIONAL ENDOWMENT FOR THE ARTS

Zephyr Press is a non-profit arts and education 501(c)(3) organization that publishes literary titles that foster a deeper understanding of cultures and languages. Zephyr books are distributed to the trade by Consortium Book Sales and Distribution [www.cbsd.com] and Small Press Distribution [www.spdbooks.org].

Cataloging-in-Publication Data is available from the Library of Congress

First Printing in 2010

ZEPHYR PRESS
50 Kenwood St.
Brookline, MA 02446

INTRODUCTION

If you know Duo Duo's writing, you most likely know him as a poet, as one among a new generation of young writers who stepped out from the spiritual badlands of the Cultural Revolution to reinvent literature as they knew it. When he began to write around 1972 at age twenty-one, it was a punishable offense to be caught with the type of poems Duo Duo was creating: deeply personal, cryptic, and often inspired by the likes of Charles Baudelaire, Marina Tsvetaeva, Sylvia Plath, and other western moderns he discovered squirreled away in caches of banned books, or passed from hand to hand in tattered volumes and hand-copied manuscripts. A certain magic resonated in this forbidden language, not just because it was fine poetry, but because public language outside Duo Duo's furtive literary circle was saturated by state politics, forced into the mold of political exhortation that took the form of slogans, songs, *Quotations from Chairman Mao*, and endless recitation of political cant at factories, schools, and on the streets. All the same, poetry was not in short supply. One could even say that it was a poetic age. But this was poetry of the grand political sublime assembled from a catalogue of approved imagery: the gloom of the "old society," the brightness of "New China," the raging tempest of the Revolution, the bright red blood of the martyrs . . . and above all the Helmsman, the Pole Star, the Sun itself, Mao Zedong. No doubt, the lyric energy of the era drove Duo Duo and his contemporaries in China's tiny poetic underground during these years, but in poetry they also found a way to tamper with language and make it their own. With the thaw of 1978, the poetry they had been circulating below state radar surfaced, was attacked, held on, and over a decade or more found its way into the canon of China's post-Mao literary history.

But the reason Duo Duo has become one of the most respected Chinese poets over the past several decades is not because he was a pathbreaker, although he was, or because his poems have been enshrined in anthologies published in China and beyond, which they have. Duo Duo matters because he has never compromised with convention—that cozy, familiar gathering place of the collective imagination where meaning is always close at hand. Instead, like most poets worthy to be called such, Duo Duo's poems recreate places where he has been physically, emotionally, and intellectually, but do so only after pulling apart and reconstructing the language handed down to him. Because of his refusal of convention, as readers we can feel quite alone when we enter these poetic places and struggle to find our own signposts through evocative and ambiguous words that, true to the genre of the lyric, seem to stand aloof from the everyday world.

This volume introduces a somewhat different, lesser-known facet of Duo Duo's literary talent. The six translated stories gathered here were originally published in Chinese in leading literary journals in China during the 1980s, and in the overseas journal *Today* (*Jintian*) in the early 1990s. All of them open new doors into the imaginary places Duo Duo has created. As fictional narrative, rather than purified lyric, these stories will seem more direct and concrete than the fragmentary music of his poems. Often the places he takes us can seem very real, like his hometown of Beijing as it experienced the political convulsions of the socialist era, the ancient city of Xi'an during the bustling 1980s, or the tidy streets of Toronto and the placid wooded islands of Lake George. Other places blur the borders of reality and fantasy, such as Duo Duo's seaside town of Wearmouth in northern England, where different temporalities, languages, and geographies converge without regard for standard boundaries of countries or consciousness. Then there is the scenery to be found nowhere other than in the realm of dream: the schizophrenic salon in the snowbound house of "Sumo," or its depopulated counterpart in the vast and empty snow plain of the title story in this collection.

Wherever they take us, all the stories are bound together by a mutable "I" through whom Duo Duo's narrators speak and perceive. Autobiographical elements are certainly at work. For instance, the detached but moving voice he adopts in his most realistic-seeming story, "Childhood, Boyhood, Youth," sketches out a life whose contours would appear to follow those of Duo Duo's own. Born Li Shizheng in 1951 as the son of a high-ranking official in Beijing, Duo Duo was like many writers of his generation. He was a child of New China who came of age amid all its contradictions: the privilege of intellectual stimulation in a well-connected household, the persecution of neighbors and fathers during the political campaigns of the 1950s and 1960s, and the anarchic freedom of being a young man during the Cultural Revolution through the 1970s. In the 1980s, as a journalist for the Beijing-based *Farmer's News*, he more than likely did travel by train . . . or was it by plane? . . . between China's big cities, much like the protagonist in "The Day I Got to Xi'an." The distinctive scenery of England

and Canada appear in these stories as well, and both are places Duo Duo lived and wrote, after he left China in the fateful year of 1989.

That year, 1989, represents an unwritten divide among these six stories. As it happened, Duo Duo witnessed the violence centered upon Tiananmen Square on the evening of June 3, then boarded a plane the following morning to fly to London for what was meant to be a short visit to read his poetry. It was fifteen years before he returned. During that decade and a half, he became a Dutch citizen and continued to write while teaching or in residency at universities in the Netherlands, the United Kingdom, and Canada. The two "exile" stories from this period, "Going Home" and "Vacation," show us Duo Duo's peripatetic creativity again at the center of imagined landscapes, foreign now, and with an even greater emphasis on the instability of his narrating "I." To read "Going Home" in particular means experiencing the makeshift, divided self that to some degree inhabits all of Duo Duo's stories. It is a narrative that turns on the insistent desire to tell one's own story in the face of overwhelming circumstances. For Duo Duo, storytelling seems to mean reserving the right to search for, but still deny, an illusion of wholeness when ones existence is inevitably fragmented, to admit to being simultaneously where you are and where you are not, to locate the past in the present and the far in the near, and find fullness in the assertion that we ought never be completely sure just where the here and the now really are.

In a perverse way, the ambiguities we find in Duo Duo's fiction can clarify our vision. You might read these stories to learn about China. The market for such knowledge is strong, and there is no shortage of people writing to make sense of that vast and rapidly changing place in the by now familiar terms of astonishing economic growth, disturbing injustices, grand spectacle, and resilient people. Duo Duo's contribution is to remind us that the fullness and coherence we seek in knowledge not just about China, but about anywhere and anything, is itself fraught with illusion, because the coherence of what we perceive of the world depends upon nothing more than the illusion of a coherent self. Like his traveler on the snow plain our greatest, if unrecognized, desire is to find and fashion for ourselves a fixed and orderly home in the wilderness, a place where we can settle in comfortably, safe from the deadly chaos on all sides. Yet wherever and whomever we are, others have come before us, others whose bodies and voices still haunt and divide, whether we perceive them or not.

John A. Crespi

SNOW PLAIN

STORY OF A SNOW PLAIN

Just two people in an expanse of five hundred kilometers.

So cold.

I had just left the cabin, fixing a brass lock on the door when the frigid air shot up through my legs into my leather overcoat. After three hours on the road my limbs had become wooden posts, no longer a part of my body. No wind, not a creature in sight. Sparse vegetation dotted the snow plain like clusters of matchsticks. I followed the trail of wagon ruts over snow that God's horse cart had crushed to a bright, smooth, almost abstract translucence. I had not packed food or books in the sack slung over my shoulder. Back at the cabin I had shaved off my beard. But beyond that, nothing I carried would keep growing. I brought no money, of course. That was something that had long since fallen into disuse, and I knew, even as I hung the lock on the door, I would never return.

I wanted desperately to stop remembering. There was just that lock, floating before my eyes—even the cabin had ceased to exist.

Then, forty-five kilometers out, a house appeared, the door ajar. Smoke from a cook fire streamed up out of the chimney. This is where I planned to stay. Maybe for a night, maybe longer, perhaps I would live there, with the owner, forever. I could not be sure. But with that thought I took the key to the brass lock from my pocket, closed my eyes, and tossed it out into the snow plain. Was this the right time? The decision had to be made at some time or other, so why not now, the exact moment it crossed my mind.

The sun was traveling, too, traversing the sky, flapping bright red sleeves, it seemed. I suddenly remembered my horse from some distant past, the horse I had ridden, had driven ahead of me, and had led by the halter just as I used to tug my father along by his sleeve. It flashed before my eyes: a pond bright with youth, the neck and mane of a horse moving through water . . .

What else had been mine?

There was a blank space left behind after all of my worries had been lifted. It did not occur to me whether I had eaten that morning or not. I wrapped the leather coat tightly around me. The fur completely worn away, the coat has become stiff and glossy from the cold. It refused to conform to my body, hardening willfully to its original form—horsehide.

At last the house came into sight: another cabin, encircled by a brilliant white wall of snow. I could not find a way in through the wall. I plunged my fist into the snow again and again—a mass of silent blows. I cried out: "Is anyone there?"

The very idea of having to shout these words aloud infuriated me.

It only proved what I already knew: there was no one inside.

To get into the cabin I would have to climb the wall of snow. Up I went.

Straddling the crest of the wall, I could see a large lock on the cabin door. I sat on the wall—one leg in, one leg out— thinking about how I had just thrown the other key into the snow. Most likely it would not have fit. But it was, after all, made to open locks. I jumped down, leaned close to a window, and wiped the glass. I punched it in. The interior was filled with snow. For a better look I smashed in all four windows: it was completely filled with snow. I kicked in the door. This was indeed a cabin of snow.

It would seem that whoever had abandoned it was even more thorough than I.

To return forty-five kilometers home through the darkness would be impossible. I had to set to work immediately to survive my first night here. By now my body was so cold I felt it could levitate from the leather overcoat. First the snow had to be cleared away. Then I would take down the doors, break them into planks, burn them for heat.

As I was clearing it out, I discovered that this cabin was much more than an empty storehouse of snow. One by one, traces of the owner's life—things I would need to survive— began to emerge. First a set of chimes.

And there was more, much more. Someone I had never seen, who had never mattered to me, and whom I had never remembered nor forgotten—the owner—a woman. A corpse.

She lay in bed. The cabin was the tomb he had left for her, with snow to cover her, and the surrounding wall of snow her gravestone. She was harder than the frozen earth. I brushed the snow off her face just as I would from a tabletop. I could not decide if she was attractive. I needed to haul her outside, to make her bed my own.

When the hands of the wall clock pointed to 11:58, I had a new home, along with a woman who had been dead for I knew not how long.

There was no need to break up the doors for fuel. The room was equipped with everything I required: firewood in a neat stack, matches, candles, liquor, tobacco, and some rabbit and deer meat, fresh-frozen, just like the woman. I sat in a wooden chair spread over with an animal pelt, facing the blazing fireplace and heating a kettle of tea. I had stopped up the four windows with dogskin bedding, and the woman was out in the yard, stiff and upright, facing the intense cold of the night sky.

I belched beef, pickled vegetables and strong liquor (I could almost recall the brand). The tobacco was quite good, and left a slight burning sensation in my nose. Hung on the wall were a hunting rifle, a long belt knife, and a fishing pole. The cellar held enough food for a lifetime. I gazed with satisfaction at everything I had chanced upon: it was a gift. Then I started to dream of a future. I would bury the woman's corpse in the ground and plant a tree over her; I would knock down the snow wall and replace it with a wooden fence; I would patch the roof, whitewash the walls, launder the bedding, and adjust the strap on the hunting rifle to fit my own shoulder. I had it all planned out. This was a gift I accepted with pleasure.

But it all hardly seemed to matter when compared to the dream that soon followed:

Life returned to the dead woman. We settled into contented domesticity. I put my hand to the plow and she worked the loom. I even saw us driving a sledge into a prosperous town to adopt a black puppy with a patch of white on its forehead . . . a scene touching, and distant . . .

And so when a rapping at the door startled me awake late that night, I simply replied, "I'm coming." Then, suddenly, it occurred to me: that was my future, out there, beyond the door.

"Who is it? Who are you?"

There was no reply.

"Who are you?!"

I asked again, and again, to no one but myself, I suppose.

By the dying light of the stove I grabbed the rifle. I would not back down. Even if the owner himself had returned, this house was now mine, and I would not relinquish my rights. I would not be forced to continue my trek across the cold and barren snow plain.

And if it truly was the owner?

"Tell me who you are or I won't open the door. Keep knocking and I'll shoot!"

The knocking continued. I did not shoot.

Standing in only my underwear, I realized my own denial. If it was a second housebreaker out there, well, then I had been the first. There was no way around it: the deed was done, yes? I fired.

The bullet pierced the ceiling.

The knocking went on, calmly and firmly.

I kicked the door hard.

It fell open with a hollow thud . . .

Clean moonlight and crisp air. Gunsmoke stole out the doorway. With the rifle at my hip I stared intently into an absolute calm. On the silvery snow the woman's corpse stood poised and alone. Once dead, dead forever. I stood in the doorway on the balls of my feet, the gun held level. Then behind me, from deep within the cabin, a voice resonated:

"That is my gun. Put it down."

. . . faint and far away, the sound of bells on a horse-drawn sledge. Daylight flooded the room. I leapt to my feet and scrambled to put on my shirt and trousers at the same time, my left arm down a shirt-sleeve as my right leg plunged into my pants. Brass bells swaying briskly on a horse's neck; I saw this clearly in my mind's eye and understood: they would soon arrive.

The bride looked exactly like the dead woman.

The driver could only be the unseen man.

I remembered: on this day I was to be married.

And that is why, as I dashed from the cabin, one hand holding up my trousers and the other shading my eyes to look into the distance, a lingering apprehension made me glance back to look for the latch ring on the door. Then I looked up. There was my bride, dressed in white with a wreath of flowers in her hair, sitting in the sledge and beckoning. She waved so urgently . . . like that big brass lock of yours.

Translated by John A. Crespi

CHILDHOOD, BOYHOOD, YOUTH

Mention Father and I remember a small, thin, calm man, standing punctually at the radio each morning listening to the weather forecast, drinking unsweetened coffee, never forgetting to change into his overshoes, walking to the office with an umbrella under one arm. Returning home in the evening he would be visibly older. His job was to lean over a desk, smoking one cigarette after another, and analyze mysterious numbers until he could foresee a world economic crisis. Maybe his job really was special, considering how dry and intense, how solemn his face looked when he was at his desk. He lived like that, too, doing everything systematically. Upon returning home from work he would give me a smile and go wash his hands, then put on his glasses, read the headlines, remove his glasses to massage his temples, eat dinner, and immediately afterwards brush his teeth (something, I can tell you, he never once neglected to do). Then he would put on his overcoat and go out for a fifteen-minute stroll—no more, no less. Back at home he would give me another smile, hum a few bars of Schubert or Mendelssohn, switch on the desk lamp, light up one of the cigarettes he had just bought down the street, and smoke late into the night. If I got up from bed to pee he would still be at his desk concentrating on his intense, solemn, very special work. The following morning he would again drink his black coffee and walk to the office. In the afternoons he napped on a cot at the office, covering his feet with the checked blanket that I had used in kindergarten.

That was my father, and I was in awe of him. Mother would always say, "Daddy is tired, he works hard. Don't bother him."

Mother was something else altogether. My respect for her was never a mere formality, even though she was forever terrorizing me by chasing me from room to room and smacking me around. All the same, I was drawn to her, if only to wear her down, press my demands for this and that, or stir up trouble. If she hit me I just loved her all the more. It's hard to imagine how someone could live without a mother, without all those foolish motherly ways.

They say that childhood memories are the most lucid, and I can't dispute that. But I don't remember much about my father.

* * * *

One evening, when I was crying for some reason, this Father of mine walked up and took me by my grimy little hand, probably to sit me down for a talk. I felt like I had been wronged, and a strong sense of shame. I don't know why, but I never got used to Father's gentleness (was it because I saw so little of him?). All he had to do was to show some emotion and I would immediately feel awkward. I was afraid of him, but it was a fear I never understood, no matter how hard I tried.

"Look, son." He was gazing at the sky.

I looked, too. What was it?

"See, the swallows have come back home."

"Where are they?"

"Over there, right over there."

Father pointed his finger into the evening sky. Through my tears I looked blearily upward. Is that it? All I saw was a blur of floaters tracing the movements of my eye.

"Do you see it?"

"Unh hunh." I wasn't so sure. "It's a swallow?"

"That's right, a swallow. . . . They've come back home,

they're good little birds." Father seemed somehow moved. "Such good little birds!"

That's what they were, swallows. Swallows don't cry, so they're good little birds.

From this I was to understand that Father didn't like children who cried. I became even more reluctant to show my feelings to Father. But was that really what he meant? I still don't know.

* * * *

The zoo was closing for the day.

As darkness fell over the grounds, the animal world came into its own. I was sandwiched between my parents, holding Mother's hand (of course, it wouldn't have been Father's) as I listened to the lions and tigers roar; it was chilling, disturbing, and every few steps I would ask Father:

"Why are they making so much noise?"

He would always reply: "They're hungry, they want to eat."

Oh. They're hungry, they want to eat, and they want to burst out of their cages, too! Should we go home? Let's go back to the Aviary for a bit. I tore myself free from Mother's hand and ran there at top speed.

"Mr. Mynah, what time is it? What time is it, Mr. Mynah?" Patiently I began calling to Mr. Mynah, over and again.

Mr. Mynah couldn't talk. Mr. Mynah wasn't real. Mr.

Mynah was carved from wood. Mother asked, too:

"What time is it, Mr. Mynah?"

Mr. Mynah remained silent, perched dumb and wooden on the tree branch.

Then it was Father's turn to ask.

"Eight o'clock, eight o'clock!"

What a wonderful voice! Low and deep, just like Father's.

"Eight o'clock, eight o'clock!"

I was ecstatic. Father could speak a language from another world!

"Eight o'clock, eight o'clock!"

Mr. Mynah rambled on in his bass voice.

Father was the only one it would talk to.

From that moment on I admired Father.

* * * *

But it was the time I was sick that his power as a father was most apparent. Outside the rain poured down. Thunder rumbled in my ears. I lay in my child's bed with a high fever. I dreamt all kinds of things: In one I saw myself as an even smaller child spending a Sunday on a lawn with Father and Mother; in another an auntie gave me a toy duck on wheels that went "quack quack" and was filled with cookies; in another the older boy next door took me to watch ice hockey and then carried me home over his back so that his shoulder got damp from my drool. And there were more: Some people charged up to "inspect" our house, not stopping till they had searched through every brick of coal; in one our neighbor (a kind old man) got taken away, with clothes draped over his wrists, so that no one could see he'd been "cuffed"; and then there were those people who had moved out of our courtyard forever, like the old lady who played piano, and the older boy who had given me ice cream, taken me out in a rowboat, carried me on his back . . .

I dreamt on, the gray-haired nursemaid beside me murmuring:

"There, there, your daddy will be back from work soon and everything will be fine."

I was unconscious when he got back from "work." Father carried me in his arms through the rain to the hospital downtown. Rainwater drip-dropped off his hat onto the raincoat wrapped snugly around me. His body gave off that odor men have when they're damp, a warm odor, unfamiliar yet soothing. Through the blur of my fever I thought: Isn't he wonderful? Isn't it wonderful to be a daddy?

When I came to (by then it was the next day) a hand was stroking my forehead. A strong feeling surged up through my heart.

"Mom!"

Mother kissed me savagely, holding me to her so tightly I could hardly breathe. "Do you feel better now, darling?"

"Mom!"

I wanted to ask, Is Father back yet?

"My little darling, Mommy brought you some tangerines."

Again she wrapped me tightly in her arms, and I was her good little boy, and she cared for me and loved me, even though I was thinking about Father.

"Mom . . ."

I wasn't going to say what I was thinking. I wanted to keep my love for Father to myself. But he still hadn't gotten home from work.

At last Father came home. At last I had wished him home. I heard his heavy breathing. Minutes passed. I could hear the water drip-dropping off his rain hat, but was afraid to open my eyes. Surely he would lean over to kiss me, and then I would tell him about the warm feeling in my heart. But he didn't lean over me. He just remained standing, quietly beside my bed. Even more time passed, until I was nearly in tears. All I heard was the strike of a match. Then he moved softly into the next room.

Later, and this is something I never told him, I cried in secret, bitterly and alone—Father, can't you see that I love you? Never again after that did I open my heart to him about anything.

I've come to a conclusion about Father, that my fear of him was real precisely because he never hit me, not once. Mother? She would kiss me all the time, and beat me just as often. And she and Father quarreled constantly, though I never heard Father raise his voice. Mother would be smashing all of her little knick-knacks, shouting and cursing at Father. Sometimes she would lunge and swing at him with whatever came to hand, mussing his hair. Father would just sit in his chair, without a word, which only goaded Mother into more of a rage. After a while, a very long while, she would tire and lose interest, pick up a comb, put her hair back in order, and study herself in the mirror. Before the day was over she would buy more things to replace what she had smashed, all of them different from before. Only then would my troubled little heart settle back in place. Is there anything that hurts a child more than watching parents fight? Back then I always felt as if I were the "guilty" one. Each time, after Mother's rage subsided, Father, who had weathered it all from his chair, would stand up, put on his overcoat, and slowly fasten each button. Then, after giving me an apologetic look, he would go out.

No one knew where.

He would come back by evening. Then Mother would set to work easing the tension in the air, little by little, with pointless chatter and jokes. Again Father would sit in his chair, gazing out the window. Several days later his solemn expression would remain unchanged. I was afraid to ask him anything, or speak to him at all, and so was Mother.

Eventually life at home would carry on as ever. My parents would make up, though each time Father's eyes seemed to grow more somber. I never knew what lay behind all their quarreling. But I felt something hidden in Father, some sort of abyss that remained from a past I could not understand, something that had robbed him of an ability to give himself to anything but his work and his evening strolls, making it impossible for him to have a real conversation with anyone. Father never had friends come over to the house; all my "uncles" and "aunties" were friends of my Mother. I remember Father's friends visting when I was very young, but at some point, I don't know why, they simply vanished. Was he thinking about them in that chair? It troubled me, and stirred my resentment, that cold detachment of Father's.

I'd have to guess that Father's secret was somehow at the root of Mother's domineering and nagging. It wasn't just her, either. Each time that reckless, arrogant older brother of mine came home, he would shut himself up in a room with Father for hours and hours. It seemed to me that my brother, a soldier, was agonizing over something, and that this something was Father. He always came and left in a hurry, for no other purpose than to speak with Father. His brows were always tightly knit from the effort of thinking up ever more piercing questions to ask. He inevitably left deeply disappointed (he was posted in another part of the country). For the past several years he hasn't been in touch at all. But at least someone in the family was impartial, and by that someone, I mean me. I always felt that even if you added up Mother and Brother, they weren't in the right any more than Father was. So why did they have to torture him like that? It was all well beyond the knowing of a child.

* * * *

Later, without really noticing, I grew up.

First I went to elementary school, was a mid-captain (or maybe it was only a lower captain), was selected as a "three-goods" student (this I'm sure about), then tested into middle school, applied myself well enough, and got average grades—all in all, nothing to brag about. I began spending more of my time outside. Father was becoming an old man, but I couldn't be bothered to notice. Like the other older children, I was more interested in seeing who was taller, who had longer legs, and dreaming about becoming a sports star. How had Father gotten to be so old in that same armchair? How had his hair turned gray leaning against the headrest of that old chair? I never once gave it any real thought. In short, our conversations became more and more infrequent, though he would occasionally offer a few stray words of encouragement, and like all fathers, had high hopes for his son. When I didn't show him my report card, Father never asked to see it, which I knew meant that he had confidence in me (and which was why I always secretly got Mother's signature when I failed a class). And Father never lectured me, not once, which deeply satisfied me as a gesture of respect. Mother was changing, too. She never lost her old habit of beating and scolding me, but when she wanted to give me a really good slap on the head she now had to search around for a stool first. One time she really smacked me right across the cheek, and then locked me in my room. It's still unclear to me why she did it. But this time I decided I wasn't going to take it like a child anymore. I tied a rope to the balcony and left a note on the desk:

"I'll still call you Mom, but I'm never coming back. You should be ashamed."

I did come back, mostly because the next morning Father was standing silently in the doorway of my friend's house. Before I had fully awoken from that blissful dream of running away, Father had set himself gingerly down at the head of the bed. I remember saying just one sentence:

"All right Dad, let's go home."

In the early morning light my friend watched father and son heading home. He always remembered that morning, he would tell me afterwards.

Mother pressed my head tightly to her breast, crying bitterly, and laughing:

"Son."

"Mmmnh. Mom."

"Is it really that shameful for a Mommy to hit her own little boy?"

"It is when that boy is already grown up."

Mother continued to beat her son without mercy, because

he was growing up all wrong. I really didn't know when it would end, though I suppose there was some good in it, since it gave her a reason to love me.

* * * *

If only she had kept hitting me forever.

And who could have imagined that she was being beaten, too?

The telling has to begin from a specific time.

All I remember now is that it happened suddenly, and was my first look at a dead person. The corpse (a woman) lay face up on the athletic field at school. She was covered by a mat, which people kept lifting to peek underneath. I caught just a glimpse: the pale, naked belly was swollen tight as a drumskin, flies crawled all over her face, her eyes were still open wide . . . then, and it all happened so fast, when I got back from school a jeep pulling a trailer was parked at the entrance to our house. Trunks sealed with paper strips, the doors of the wardrobe flung open, clothes hanging out of the drawers, the floor strewn with photographs, letters, and smashed phonograph records. There were wisps of mother's hair, and a cigarette holder, snapped in half, which was Father's. The jeep drove off. The old cat they had chased away came back home.

From then on I was an adult.

I and the other children who had grown up overnight, children with vague shadows of moustaches just visible above our lips, dressed up in our fathers' woolen overcoats and tunic suits. Father's silver cigarette case, his lighter, and all the things that had been in fashion when he was young, armed us for the present. These objects went with us everywhere—the street corners, the ice rink, the bars . . . picking fights, swilling booze, pulling leather caps down over our eyes or cocking them back on our heads, cruising on bicycles, chasing our enemies, getting into rumbles, meeting up at someone's house, bicycles lined up outside, thundering upstairs in our heavy leather boots, then swinging our feet up onto a table to smoke, play cards, drink hard. Then flashlight beams, an urgent pounding at the door, we'd dash out to the balcony and scramble over one another to leap to our escape . . .

I learned what it meant to squander one's days, to let youth slip away . . .

* * * *

That's how it went until two years ago, when I went to see Father out in the countryside.

My father in the countryside? Nothing strange about that. Whose father wasn't out in the country? Ah, and I forgot to mention that long before he went there I was long gone from Beijing. I was off with those friends of mine, sleeping on an earthen kang in a farm village, rolling cigarettes, telling fortunes and ghost stories, lying in the warm sun, shouldering bundles of straw, divvying up grain rations. So many years had gone by. What was Father like now? Where was Mother? The only thing I remembered was the old live-in nursemaid who had reared me for fifteen years. She had left long ago, back to her hometown. Once she made the long trip just to see me, but I didn't even let her in the door. Why not? I could make no sense of what I was feeling. When I heard her going down the stairs my heart became stone.

I went to see Father. On the way there I came down with acute bilious hepatitis. I hadn't had personal contact with any sort of disease since I'd become an adult, much less did I understand the danger. They treated me for malaria.

By that time, Father's hair had turned completely white. We rode a tractor over a dirt road in the countryside, headed from the county hospital to the barracks where Father was living with the others. I was burning up with fever. Any healthy person would have been feverish, too, since the temperature outside was 44 or 45 degrees celsius. If he hadn't taken me to see the doctor, Father would have been on the job, firing bricks at a kiln.

After we had climbed down off that maddeningly hot tractor, a long walk still lay ahead of us. Just thinking about it almost made me black out. A sudden, powerful wave of anger came over me. Here I was locked in the invisible grip of this demon disease, while right beside me stood a perfectly healthy person who, even though he was my father, or perhaps because of it, aroused my loathing. I felt sad, wounded. I hated it all.

I started cursing, a non-stop stream of the foulest words I could muster. I'd have to say Father had never heard this type of language coming from his own son's mouth, and maybe he couldn't believe what he was hearing. I cursed the weather, the sun, the length of the road, and those goddamned puny southern trees. I cursed everything, just to provoke my father's disgust, to declare to his face the right I now possessed as an adult to curse freely and fluently. The old man was going to hear everything I'd learned!

But he didn't say anything. Maybe he'd already seen it coming on. He ought to be carrying me on his back! What was wrong with him? He ought to take this young guy up on his stooped and frail old back! But he was silent—the old fart! I began goading him with a rude stare, but all I saw in his old eyes was a greater tolerance, or even humility. For an instant I felt I should forgive the old man. I'd lost the outlet for my anger. The man beside me became no more than a useless, decrepit father. I felt my strength draining away even as my rage mounted.

"I can't walk, I can't!"

"Rest a bit, then."

"Rest?!"

"All right . . ."

"All right?!"

I fought back my anger, afraid I truly might go mad. But immediately I tore into him again: "Take it away! You and this godforsaken place—get it away from me!"

"......"

Father no longer had those same ways of helping me pull through like he used to, like he did when I was small. With the county hospital over twenty kilometers away, the only option was to go to his barracks and dab on some mercurochrome. For now, Father just sat down calmly, because I was still lying there on the road, fuming. He let the sun shine cruelly on his bald pate. I was wearing his straw hat.

Strange. He wasn't sweating.

Bastard.

I stared balefully ahead, down a road that trailed dizzily into an endless space. I snatched the straw hat from my head and twisted it in my hands for all I was worth. It crackled and split into pieces. Father looked out ahead, saying nothing.

"You're a disgrace!"

My madness surged again. My saliva sputtered onto the ground and onto my feet.

"You're a disgrace!"

Father didn't flinch. Not a trace of disquiet showed in his face.

His composure infuriated me all the more. "Do you understand what I'm saying to you!?"

"Let's go! We don't have a choice—I'll walk till I drop dead, goddammit!"

I hauled myself up and started to walk. Father followed.

I walked in big, staggering strides, leaving him behind. I'd gone just a few steps before I sat down hard on the ground again, bruising myself painfully and bringing a flood of hot, humiliating tears to my eyes. I sat down dead center in the road; if a truck happened to come along I would simply ram it with my head.

Father came hurrying up and sat at the edge of the road, gazing at me silently, analyzing my pain as if he were some sort of servant.

Evening came. We sat together in the darkness.

We started walking again, all the way to our destination.

* * * *

Father hung the mosquito netting and set a glass of glucose solution by the head of my bed (I had actually brought it for him, since I knew the sort of thing he normally had to eat out here gave him indigestion). The doctor came and left. He gave me one shot, and then several more misdiagnosed shots that could have killed me. I was lying on my back, battling barehanded against the invisible enemy inside my body. I chewed a hole through the mosquito netting and let all the mosquitoes in to sting, bite, and suck my blood, then I scratched until every inch of me was a bleeding mess. The time passed in a semi-conscious stupor, like a nightmare that wouldn't end. At some point I heard the roar of a malevolent voice:

"Idiot! Bastard!"

Was it me cursing again?

"Clean it up, now! Get moving, you idiot!"

"Yes, right away. I'll clean it up. Tomorrow . . ."

It was Father's voice. But that other voice . . .

I had no idea whose it could be, but I was sure I had heard it somewhere before . . .

* * * *

How many years earlier had it been? Winter had come, and I was sending clothes to Father. Just as I arrived at the door of his room I heard a ferocious voice (not the exact same voice as later, but the same sort of voice):

"What! Bastard! Talk back, will you?!"

I felt a tightening sensation around my heart.

"Get along, you old fart!"

I pushed open the door and went in. The old man was kneeling silently on the floor tying a bundle of books. Beside him stood a burly man, his leather shoes planted threateningly next to Father's hands.

"Get up! Up, up!"

The big man viciously kicked the old man's legs.

The old man suddenly saw me, saw my face livid and my fists clenched and quivering. The old man got up and stood between me and the other man.

"Is this your son?"

"Yes. He brought me some things."

"What did he bring you, you old scoundrel!"

Blood rushed to my eyes.

The old man pressed his body tightly against mine.

"Look here—give it to him and then leave."

The big man tossed his cigarette butt on the floor and went out.

Father didn't turn around to face me, didn't raise his head, didn't say a word to me. It wasn't the first time this sort of thing had happened. Just as every child's father might get beaten up, every household might have its doors sealed, or every father's neckties might be tied to a pole to make a mop . . . there's really no point in talking about it.

Father slapped the dust from his knees. I noticed he was wearing a work uniform. This made me think of a day not very long ago when I was out cruising on bicycles with a group of kids, hooting and charging through the streets like we owned them. A garbage truck suddenly started rolling toward us. Someone on it caught my attention. He was wearing a work uniform with a beat-up cloth cap, and looked vaguely familiar. The smile vanished from my face; it was Father. Ever since, those big steel shovels on the truck have lodged in my memory, floating into my mind's eye from time to time, just like a memory one of my buddies told me he'd once had: Turning the corner into his alley on the way back from school one day, he spotted something in the distance flashing in the sunlight. He quickly understood. It was his family's big wardrobe, loaded high on the bed of a truck, waiting to be taken away. That wardrobe mirror stabbed into his memory, leaving a permanent wound. . . .

"Go back, son."

"Uh huh."

I had never been so well behaved as I was on that day. I wanted to take Father's hand.

"How's the old cat doing?"

All Father ever asked about was the old cat. It was still alive. I still had it. Mother had left Father years ago. Even so, she still worried about him. I knew Father never gave up on the idea that one day she would come to understand him.

How much longer did that ferocious voice continue? I don't know.

All I knew was that I must have vomited, made a mess of the place, causing someone to reprimand Father, to make him mop it up and put everything back in order. When I opened my eyes it was almost dawn. Clearly Father had sat up the entire night, waiting quietly for me to regain consciousness. We were silent for a long time in the early morning sunlight. It was this stretch of time, this wordless stretch of time, that the wall between us fell away. Father lifted my hand and pressed something into it: bank notes (it was everything he had).

"Go back, as soon as you can."

"Uh huh."

"Go straight back to Beijing. Do not stop anywhere else."

"Uh huh."

* * * *

We were back on the road we had walked the day before.

The morning breeze was soothing, but memory made me afraid to speak. Father's years of authority had been utterly swept away, all by my own doing, and yet I had never respected him more than I did right then.

Father sent me all the way to the tractor headed for the city.

I clambered aboard the thundering machine. Father stood down below.

I avoided his eyes until the very last moment. The tractor started moving. I suddenly noticed an odd expression on Father's face, a look so very unfamiliar that in my entire life I only saw it that one time. . . . Ah, Father, Dad, you wouldn't . . .

Tears streamed down my cheeks. Father was left behind. He was growing smaller, ever smaller. I could still see his white hair tossed gently by the morning breeze. Father was left behind, forever. Again he would walk back to the barracks by himself along the little country paths, face a world of oppression and intimidation. But never again would he have the company, and the hatred, of his son. . . .

That's how it was the last time I saw Father.

No. The last time I saw Father was a year ago.

Just as before there was that narrow country road, and just as before we went on foot. Only now it was no longer Father and I, but me and Mother. The damp gloom of the southern winter felt saturated with a cold hostility. It was our family reunion.

They had laid Father out on a big blackboard. When they opened the padlock on the door to the shed, Mother's legs grew weak. She leaned into me. Someone pulled aside the shroud. There was Father's face. The shroud was drawn back over him very quickly. Then they carried him away on the blackboard, shouldered his body onto a tractor, and drove off.

"There is a very deep well near the barracks." That was all they told us. We didn't have to believe any of it, except one thing: it was over.

A year passed. I still saw Father's face from time to time, and each time I saw in his eyes a disbelieving, anxious look, a look that called up the memory of someone else, also a father, but not my own. I had seen the same disbelief, the same questioning, in that other father's eyes. It had been a brutal scene. Those eyes scanned the faces of everyone standing in front of him, including my own.

"Hold it right there! Don't move!"

That poor soul, that father, had been an old man, too, the dean of our school. Out on the athletic field that August day he was balancing a mess tin filled with boiled water on his head. For five seconds he managed to hold it there. When the water spilled, a leather belt instantly landed on his body. He howled, his face contorting, his eyes filled with terror, rage, but most of all, shock. It was a scorching look of agony, panicked and searching. Onto his head went another mess tin of boiled water. Again he cried out, a second pair of hands snatched the leather belt and lashed out at him even harder. The old man writhed on the ground, shouting and pleading as each person from the crowd of onlookers fought for their chance to kick him, to punch him. The most savage, the most forceful of them all was the one who had snatched the belt away—the dean's son.

A number of years later I saw him out in the countryside. He was living alone in a house whose floor was an inch thick with pigeon shit and cigarette butts. Some time after that someone told me he had cut off his little fingers with an axe, and that he now believed in God.

Axes make me think of something else I once saw:

Another hot day. Another father was being surrounded and beaten when an eight- or nine-year-old kid suddenly charged into the crowd with a hatchet in his hands. Before he could raise it the father grabbed him. Someone kicked the child to the ground. The father sheltered the child with his own body, refusing to be separated. Leather belts and clubs rained down on the father's back. These were belts with steel buckles, clubs made from square-cut lumber; these were sturdy legs that kicked soccer balls, feet clad in sneakers; this was a father with a deeply lined face, a child with a bookbag still on his back.

When a hand grabbed the child's hair the father bit down hard, clamping that hand between his teeth. They wrenched out the father's teeth, one by one, using a pair of pliers. With bloody, mutilated gums, the father still clamped down on the hand that had reached for his son.

That hand makes me think of even more people, more places, more blood-soaked scenes. They remain in my eyes, forever indelible. When I meet Father again, the old man will see them all, and understand. . . .

Translated by John A. Crespi

SUMO

Thick snow fell along the way. I didn't know where I was going. Snowflakes dripped down from phonograph albums spinning in the heavens, notes altering the road into a long, narrow musical score.

If I said that no one else was out on the streets it'd be because I was ignoring them. There were a few stray shadows, but I didn't see anyone moving. I'd forgotten how I'd gotten to this town—actually, I'd been in it all along. Even though it was evening, the sky was bright enough to reveal everything around me. I imagined the town stretched upright, its streets like twenty crisscrossed ladders bound together. Everything appeared whitewashed; or rather, everything had lost its color. The walls along each street appeared surreal, and the windows were blocked up. I could tell they were windows because of the remaining frames. Despite being stuffed full of stones they still were called windows. This filled me with a sense of dread. Nobody was around, only things, things that remained silent. I was motivated by fear. I feared them, so I kept on walking. I had a map of the entire town etched into my mind, and I'd gone over it millions of times in my head. In reality I'd only been through about a quarter of the town. Finally someone else was moving, drawing near, coming towards me. I desperately wanted to say that this person was someone other than me, but I was quickly forced to admit that he, in fact, was precisely me. There was no other alternative.

If I were talking in my sleep, I could be forgiven for what I am now saying. But that simply is not the case. I approached a large house with a slanted roof covered in snow. A man emerged from the house. I watched him intently, but was unable to make out his features. Perhaps I was predetermined not to see him clearly. He stepped forward, moving away from the house. He walked straight away.

I did not knock. Through the half-opened door I saw a room full of people. Numerous hands reached out and pulled me inside. I did not enter on my own. I had not come there to inform them, "It's snowing all over the world."

"But you just left!"

Someone shouted this as soon as I entered the room. Then someone else tapped me on the shoulder, "Didn't you just leave?!" I was completely baffled. "Out relieving yourself?" I didn't understand, and decided not to pay any attention to them. As I was searching for an empty seat I thought I recognized a face. I turned my head to see that everyone was staring straight at me, and she among them. (But who was she?)

This is when I recovered my sense of hearing. Music was blaring. The people inside the room must have been listening to it all along. Sofas, chairs, a bed, even the windowsills were packed with bodies. I could just make out Mahler's "Das Lied von der Erde" and Ravel's "Rapsodie Espagnole." Besides the music, the room was overflowing with voices and laughter. I was back in a familiar setting—an occasional gathering of young punks. In order to stay in character I maintained a look of complete and utter apathy from the moment that I entered the room. I did not raise my head to make eye contact even once. I felt ill at ease, and then I heard "That rat had his eyes done! . . ." and then "Dammit, you're right!" This was a single page from the book of my life, and that particular "Dammit" a bookmark. I lifted my gaze slightly and, just as I expected, our eyes met. (Who did she look like?)

Judging from the conversation, I'd already figured out who she was, and who they were. Over her husband's shoulder (She already had a husband) I was, for a brief moment, gazing directly into her eyes. And then my eyes slid away from her, even more smoothly than a boat gliding past another. She continued the conversation, talking with people nearby. I could sense among the dull and boring things she was saying that there was some secret, a glass eye among a pile of buttons—a secret that had something to do with me; though, as it was of a most intimate nature, its meaning was as impenetrable as a dream. Her husband was most likely a decent enough guy, and nobody would ever consider calling him "Prick." He had an impressive head of hair, though within that head he was probably concealing sharp weapons—perhaps a mind that no longer believed in God. He had long broad shoulders capable of simultaneously embracing her and the sofa. His strength was undoubtedly boundless. He glanced at me and donned an ambiguous smile. He and his nostrils were as stupid as two bullets. Then his eyes stopped lingering on me.

I heard her bragging about her daughter. (They already had a daughter.)

"Just like her father, isn't she? Eyes like a fox, shimmering green . . ."

"That little chameleon."

"Why didn't you bring her?"

Everyday chitchat, a bit of comfort for these young punks.

I should have felt relaxed, or at least bored. But instead I realized something—something that came out of nowhere and with overwhelming intensity. She had stopped sizing me up, but I gathered that she was merely guiding me toward the past by avoiding talking about it; she was steering the conversation toward banalities. I knew her game—talk to everybody but only really talk to you; see if you hear things differently from the others.

She was talking, gathering something luminous from all of the lost years, completely absorbed in the narration. Under her spell, the entire room of attentive fools had been deceived. Then at some imperceptible moment, the music stopped, and she became the protagonist of the performance. In ridiculing her husband's red ears and her daughter's little mouse claws, she obviously had plenty of wit, the least example of which, once displayed, was enough to satisfy the imagination of each of the buffoons in the room. To her, my eyes were a form of trial since they openly revealed our shared memories. She could sense it immediately. She would always pause for a moment as a way of deflecting my conspiracy, until there was enough force to deflate my courage. After that she would continue in even more indistinct tones.

(These memories came from a family that had been consumed in a fire. I thought constantly about that place. I was crazed, but the place was not. Before the memories began there had been a person similar to her, who had attempted to abort me, to drown me before I was able to remember. I was as thin as air, for time did not yet seem to exist.)

She began to talk more quickly, more hastily—her vexations, as tiny and fragmentary as pebbles, were laid out as the path of her life, glimmering under the velvet curtain of darkness. These heart pains belong solely to women. And yet it was not all misfortune on her part, but more a lack of freedom. An exquisite chain of pure gold tied around her throat that led her along, placing her in the room where she moved among cream, roses, wine, and a bed. She was not living a life, but was being exhibited (At this point she exchanged a glance of tacit understanding with her husband), even though she was a silent rebel—a beautiful wheel, a luxurious wheel that could be exchanged for the entire edifice of a grand hotel. She effortlessly strung together stories, the audience was in the palm of her hand. She was born with these gifts. Touched by her words, I directed my gaze upon her face, her perfect face, the biggest bet I could ever expect to make in this life—the glances we exchanged foretold my entire future.

(Eyes, such a minuscule weapon within man's secret compartment, from the arsenal of memories, from her glance I came to know myself. Only those who had not yet found themselves were safe.)

She was testing my memory with a simultaneously sweet and cruel smile that hung at the corners of her mouth. A space had already been prepared in her heart to hunt me. I remained composed, hoping to remain on the outside. Just as I had done in the past, or, actually before I'd ever been born. I must not let the past flood back over me. She kept smiling, confident that I could see through her. We didn't exchange a single word, and had only known each other for fifteen or so minutes. Without needing to raise my eyes, I could tell that her husband was sizing me up from a corner of the room. I could feel his eyes, a cold sword on my back, watching both his woman and me. He didn't say a word. But I knew that he, more than anyone else, sensed that something was about to go wrong. At least I believed that he had given serious thought to the matter. He took out a cigarette case, his fingers as white as bone.

I must not have been wrong because everyone else in the room seemed to be vaguely aware of some event they were entirely ignorant of, the smell of a length of burning rubber-sheathed wire, an air of conspiracy, they had sensed (nerves that could turn a man into a devil) that there was a single thing, leaking drop by drop, some thing that they were trying to be rid of, which made them all very ill at ease. Everybody feigned introspection—all of this indicated that the thing was analogous to a cause, dripping like water between her and me. If I had wanted to remain silent, it all would have been in vain—my broad and wan forehead looked like a lethal weapon in a murderer's hand. What's more, my two eyes betrayed my resentment, which forced me to admit that I was profoundly connected to the others.

At this precise moment, her voice, which was as sonorous as a ringing bell, stopped. Every corner of the room was silent, expecting something to happen. Not a soul could remind her of where she had just stopped; in an instant nobody any longer believed that what she had been talking about was what had actually appeared within the arrangement of her words. More acute than a dog's nose, the observations, which happened to coincide, were driving them to focus their judgment upon me—they somehow had figured out that I was the cause of everything! I, the one person who had been as quiet as a dead mouse since entering. If ever there has been a moment that can be characterized as "doomed," this was that moment:

"Ah, you cheat!" I couldn't tell who the first one to point at me was. "Do we need to come over and get you?" "Is that how it's going to be!?" "It's all becoming perfectly clear now!" Countless hands pointed at me. The noise poured over my back like boiling water. From out of the thousands of voices I caught hers distinctly, "So, I've been kept waiting. I didn't realize until just now that it was you." On hearing this, I caught sight of her husband's face. He was suddenly standing right next to me, placing his hand on my shoulder. I heard his voice probing, "Keep it up and you'll really be asking for it." I raised both of my hands like I thought was being expected of me, though I didn't know what it meant. Was I refusing or giving up? I didn't really understand.

"Surely we aren't forcing you!" "Certainly not!" "We don't know him!" More vigorous cries followed (some chuckling in between) "Singer? You mean those individuals who open their mouths so wide?" I heaved a deep sigh of relief. So, I was a singer? They were asking me to do what was expected of a singer, which is, to sing. Then they uncovered the piano. Someone struck several notes, saying, "Let's hear a tune." People suddenly turned back to her again. Eager to refuse, she grasped her husband's shoulder for support. For a second it all seemed so familiar, as if it had happened once before. Had I already been through all of this? I felt like I was suffocating—awkward, bored and listless. Time had shown me its solemnity—how had I suddenly grown senile? I must have been in the room too long. I got up and headed straight for the door, not turning back to glance at her. Who was she? I didn't want to think about it anymore. She was not the first woman I had forgotten.

Outside of the house was the world. Outside of the house was the street. The street was the way. The snow was falling. I saw a man approaching. He would see me leaving. He knew I would march off on my way, and perhaps I had a destination, but would never reach it. It had already taken me so long, but since I had not yet reached it, I kept walking. But, as long as I walked, I would never reach it. Because I've never reached the beginning, I've gained nothing more than I've already had, and would be on the road forever. Perhaps he would offer me a blessing. He was getting closer. He was the same one who had gone in earlier.

He would enter the large house, cross the winding corridor in the courtyard, and come to that same door. He would find the room full of people through the half-opened door. Numerous hands would reach out to pull him inside. The doorknob was shiny, having been grasped by so many hands. From the time it was constructed until now, at least one hundred generations had lived in this house. When the door opened, he would find that the odor in the room had been accumulating for hundreds of years. Would he enjoy the lingering beauty of this house as much as he appreciated an ancient work of art? Or would he simply buy a million new bricks to build an even larger house to enclose this one?

I headed straight toward the man, only to discover that the man was also coming straight toward me. He passed by, going into the house. He walked right in.

"But you just left!"

As I came into the room someone shouted at me, "You just left!" I didn't understand what he was talking about, nor did I wish to understand. So I replied, "I just got here." Then someone else shouted, "Out relieving yourself?" "It takes fifteen years for him to wash his hands," which was followed by laughter. I didn't understand what this meant, so I simply repeated, "I just got here."

"You keep insisting that you just got here." More people were shouting at me, "Well, we certainly aren't going to force you!" "We're not!" "We will not!" After that nobody paid any more attention to me. I walked straight towards an empty seat. Then I thought I saw a familiar face. I turned. Everyone was staring at me, and she among them. But who was she? "No. I mean to say—who did she look like?) She was taxing my memory with the simultaneously sweet and cruel smile that was hanging at the corners of her mouth.

The memory came from a family that had been burned in a huge fire—whoever she was, I did remember. I remembered each of her footsteps as she was going upstairs on the tips of her shoes, had made my heart ache like a child's budding breasts; I remembered how she appeared when she laughed and laughed until the pearls and jewels trembled on her chest; I remembered that each word she precisely chose to utter bore ill intentions, each word a trap. Well, I had distinctly seen, and remembered well, that woman coiled up on the king-sized bed, whoever she was, a python with a slender waist, her nerves giving off electricity, anger. Yet how sweet was the bait, the gestures she made in the dark green lamplight! Then I remembered."

The noise grew louder. The piano had been uncovered. Someone struck several keys. "Let's have a tune!" No, no. It's unfair of you to ask. I've forgotten everything. I'm out of practice, and grown lazy. It's been fifteen years." She continued to refuse. "Technique is timeless!" "Don't keep us waiting. Please play!" People continued to woo her while she adamantly refused, holding onto a man's shoulder for support. This scene seemed instantly familiar, even repetitious. The man she was leaning against turned, smiling faintly at me; and this completed the entire scene of my memory.

As the man turned to look at me his face suddenly grew savage, his mouth revealing a pitch-dark oral cavity, teeth denuded of their enamel—like the pilings around a private estate. I recognized him. He was the true protagonist of the story, the cause of this event. And then even more dreadful words escaped from me, "There is another. Another one." I immediately realized the destructive power of these words. People were struck dumb. A minute before they had been sitting on the sofas, but now they were all standing up, their eyes focused on me. They'd heard! They'd all heard! Only they could not be sure where the voice had come from.

They soon heard it again. "There is another. Another one. It is you." He was the one who said it. The man was addressing everyone, pointing at me. I was struck again. In the innermost reaches of my mind, I was hit by a painful blow, feeling as if electricity had passed through me. I watched the man pick up his hat with one hand, supporting her waist with the other, and walk towards the door. Strikingly pale, her face gave off a strange sort of smile, like a flower that nobody had ever seen before. They left without saying good-bye. Everyone in the room stood transfixed, unable to speak of the wonder. After a while, the door was again pushed open, a crack revealed, a voice passing from outside, "He has never come back since. Because the time has not yet come. So long."

(No. They should not have gone away like that. They should not have, so indifferently, allowed me to become a calm, middle-aged man gradually putting on weight. They could not deny this. They might have avoided it. I would tenaciously clarify the past for what I did not remember. She had gone. I followed outside, only to find myself in a wilderness, holding the red scarf she had forgotten, which looked like a drop of blood shed from her body. Everything else was spotlessly white; on my left and my right, the worlds of open blankness were poised to meet and merge into each other at any moment. Yet I was still a child.)

Snow was still falling. I could hear the roof groaning under its weight. Throughout the room the deafening echoes of "The time has not yet come," resounded over and over.

"I've told you, it just isn't fair. I've forgotten. How can I do yesterday's exercises today?" She continued defending herself. "Why not!" Let's begin again!" Again I heard their voices wooing and again her refusals; again I saw the people in the room, those same people, the uncovered piano, and her husband still trying to come to her aid. I couldn't stand it any longer. I would go. As soon as this occurred to me, time promptly bared its solemnity: I had grown old. Limping on two stiff legs, I could barely reach the door. She was blocking my way. She asked, "Are you going home?" I replied, "Yes, I am going home." "Take me away." "The door is open. The door was just open. Now it is closed." "Forever?" I asked. "Forever has already been."

A sudden pause. All the people in the room jumped up as if they had suddenly gone insane, rushing towards me, encircling me. They rudely shook my shoulders and pulled at my hair; some kneed me in the stomach, and others tried to tear at my ears. Obviously this was the day when the whole truth would come out.

"What are you doing? What is it that you do each and every day?!"

"Why don't you speak clearly?"

"What are you talking about!?"

"Tell me! What are you talking about!?"

They wanted to know just one thing. Who was I? Where did I come from? Instead of answering their questions, I tried desperately to free myself from the crowd. I wanted to find out which direction they'd gone, but it was too late! They'd already escaped—in the midst of the confusion, they'd gone back out the door, she pulled by her husband's hand, her husband having picked up the hat and scarf from the sofa.

At last I roared, "They've gone! Nothing else matters!"

Flowing past me like boiling water, the ignorant crowd poured from the door. The room grew exceedingly quiet, as if the time had come, had come at last. I stood in the middle of the room, and only then did I realize that I was unable to take even one step. The floor was completely filled with sleeping bodies. They were covering the entire floor in sixes and sevens. Had they been sleeping there all along? Was it . . . I barely had time to think about this when the crowd that had rushed out now suddenly returned. They spoke very quickly and heatedly, and their words were entirely beyond my comprehension, until a man came up to me and asked:

"So what's the matter with you?"

I shrugged and said, "I didn't ask you."

"But we need to ask you."

"So, you really don't know?" I responded.

"Know what? You know! Ah, you know!"

People rushed at me again. Even those who had been lying on the floor all got up this time. They had been awake, or else they had not yet fallen asleep, or else they had not been on the floor at all—I was hopelessly confused.

"None of you here knows?"

"You scoundrel!"

I couldn't control my mouth now. My mouth was speaking

on its own—"None of you hear knows?"

I could see that the people who had gotten up from the floor appeared even more furious. I'd been intending to tell them what I knew, but I quickly realized that there was no point—they couldn't hear, and they were the people who really needed to hear. Besides, the moment had already passed, and there would never be a chance to hear it again. This was the only thing I knew. Then I laughed out loud for what I knew. Amidst the incessant laughter that I could not contain, I could not help realizing that—at that moment, I had said, I was not coming to tell them, "It's snowing all over the world." I laughed and laughed until somebody berated me loudly, "Never come back here again!" To which I chimed back, "fine."

Translated by Jiang Hong and Larry McCaffery
and revised by John A. Crespi

THE DAY I GOT TO XI'AN

I spotted the medical academy's sign from a good distance away, but then another sign leaped into view next to it—the business school's. I was about to stop one of the students to ask directions when I heard—no, saw her coming toward me with a "Hey!" Relieved now, I eased out of the big manic strides I had been taking. I walked along beside her. Suddenly, I felt as though someone had been added in between the two people here and that this other someone was me. Whatever this feeling was, it trapped inside me everything I had intended to say to her.

All I said as we walked through the medical academy was her name, Xiao Tong, in a flat, dry voice. Was I afraid of never being able to call her name again?

Inside the dormitory, clothes were hung up all over the place to dry. I had to push through at least three or four layers of laundry before I could make out the door to the inside room. Once inside we stood there, facing each other, then sat down. A bed, a desk, two chairs (one for me, one for her), a radio-cassette deck, four bare walls, and a table, which would have been bare as well if it hadn't been for the dust. Just then I noticed I'd forgotten to bring cigarettes. I hardly asked anything about her. None of the usual "How's it going?"—a commonplace I'm sick of. What does that mean, *how?* How *could* it be going? But she wasn't exactly making me feel at home either, I noticed. I rested my arms on the table, rapped out a little beat with my knuckles, crossed my legs, recrossed my legs, and knew this visit was not going to be a pleasant one. In a year and a half (she'd been transferred to the medical academy a year and a half ago), she'd had maybe four visitors. She'd gotten fat, ugly, and she was telling her favorite stories about herself. My heart sank when she said she hardly drank any water except at the three meals in the cafeteria (Sundays she often didn't go at all). Now I had no choice but to ask her to please bring me a glass of water. I was waiting for that water.

So that was about it. Then from somewhere or other, out popped that little gem of a phrase, *nervous breakdown.* She perked right up, hearing that. She hadn't slept a wink last night ("You've just *got* to get sleep after sweating heavily"). Except for lectures (she was a teacher) twelve classes a week, she slept through everything, all through those two years she didn't have classes, and on Sundays, too.

"Oh really? . . . Is that right?" When did I start humoring her like this, I wondered. It probably got this way because she had no interest at all in anything I could have said to her but was perfectly content with the way her own life was going these days. Compared with someone like me, who is always criticizing himself, who tries hard to straighten himself out, she came across as neat and composed as could be. I had the feeling, though, that she treated everyone as if he or she were her doctor. That would explain why everything we talked about had to do with pathology and why I suddenly found myself playing psychiatrist, racking my brains to come up with the most pedestrian advice: "No, that won't do. . . . No matter what, you can't go on like that. . . . You've got to do something, anything, just do it. . . . Do it along with other people . . ."

This was leading nowhere. For two hours, it was as though she were someone perpetually waiting at a bus stop, and I were the bus. No cigarettes, no water—just me trying to help an overweight, imperturbable woman try to figure out how to get her life together. I mean, I was trying to think it through for her: one way is to see that people are different, that they behave differently. She didn't make that derisory little sniff when I got on the subject of behavior, or at least I don't think I heard one, but even so the second I said the word *behave,* my confidence drained away. She was totally wrapped up in herself—her reactions had slowed, making her useless to herself and to anyone else. "So . . . you should love . . ."

I told her how I had rescued myself—that is, how I had admitted to myself that I had a problem: lonely to the edge of madness, disgusted, hiding from everyone. I told her how I missed my cat so much after it ran away that I spent a month looking for it; how every night coming into the stairwell, I would stare ravenously at my mail slot, though I couldn't remember having written to anyone, not even a simple card; and how after work, I let myself pedal my bicycle on and on, oblivious to where I was headed; and then how I finally understood something. "You should . . ."

You should help others, abandon the idea of self-worth— or rather, making your own life more worthwhile is what it's all about. One day around noon at a greengrocer's stall, I saw a boy dragging his younger sister along the ground. I broke through the crowd of indifferent onlookers, shoved the little brat away, helped the girl to her feet, and ordered the boy to take her home. I told Xiao Tong about the throb of joy I felt at doing this good turn, how from then on, I kept on doing good turns, and how I felt happier than ever before. Then I couldn't take it any longer: "Can I—may I have a glass of water?"

She was a long time registering my request. First, she said

she'd run out of tea; then she said there wasn't any water already boiled and the fire in the stove had gone out. She talked on and on, sitting there in her chair. Finally, she said, "Love?"

For the seventy-second time, I thought to myself, I've got to go. But somehow I couldn't make myself get up. The sun, three hours of whose light I'd squandered while sitting in there, had sunk down past her kitchen. In that room in the fading light, I noticed her foot had gotten fatter, too, cocked up on her knee and squeezed into a sneaker. Still, there was no way I could bring myself to say, I've got to go. In the silence, I could almost see her after I'd gone, still sitting there.

I finally did get the drink of water. I was the one who lit the stove. When the water was just about to boil, I broke the silence: "How about a stroll over to Wild Goose Pagoda?" She said it was all the same to her whether she went or not. Then another half hour of silence before I suggested again that we go to the pagoda. In the meantime, she had turned on some music, let it play for about a minute, and turned it off again. At last, I found the strength to stand up and say, "I've got to be going." Her eyes (they looked fatter, too) seemed to say that she wouldn't oppose the wishes of anyone in the world. In other words, I was free to come and go as I pleased.

We went out, and she escorted me across the campus. Some students were playing volleyball. I said I had to use the rest room. She gave me directions on how to get there. It seemed so complex: I had to turn several corners and go all the way inside some building. When I came back, she had changed her mind. (I thought that it was fine for her to have made up her mind in the first place; if she changed it back again, all the better.) I told her what I had just been thinking, and she told me that we could take a shortcut to Wild Goose Pagoda, that there were a lot of vendors selling Xi'an-style snacks near the pagoda, and that we could have for dinner some things I couldn't find in Beijing. That interested me. I didn't remind her, though, what a terrific gourmand she used to be.

I practically had to force her to decide whether or not she was going to climb the tower, and then I had to tell her three times, "If you don't want to climb it, you can wait for me at the bottom." As far as I recall, this was all we said along the way. Walking together, riding the bus, stepping off the bus, and continuing to walk on, we were locked into an acute awkwardness. She said she may as well climb the pagoda, so I went to buy a couple of tickets. Going up (seven stories in all), I wasn't sure if I should give her a hand or if we should each make our own way. I figured I'd let my elbow bump hers on the way up—that way, she could decide what to do. I kept thinking that's what I was going to do, but I may not actually have done it. Through the four windows of the pagoda's top story, we gazed out at the city and suburbs of Xi'an, spreading out as far as the eye could see. . . . If it had been just me going up the pagoda, that last phrase wouldn't have stuck in my mind.

We left Wild Goose Pagoda and walked along at a moderate pace. "Shall we get something to eat?" She seemed to have forgotten about the eating part. Neither of us was hungry at all, but we each had a deep-fried dried persimmon. All I could think about was rushing to the bus station and getting away from her as soon as possible. Then, of all things, she started going on about how there used to be so many snack vendors around this place, but now there's hardly anything except for stuff like bean noodles. As for me, I was still thinking of the twenty cents I'd spent on those two dried persimmons. She said she knew of a good restaurant near Dachai Market, but didn't say if she thought we should go or not. I said, "Let's head over there." We headed over.

Dachai was bustling and brightly lit. She led me into a food shop selling pastries. I asked her, "What's the point of coming in here?" So we went right out again and started on a search for that unfindable restaurant. Already it was seven-thirty, and most of the restaurants had shut down. The red faces of drinkers careened out of restaurant doors. We kept on, walking from street to street with no idea what we were after. All I could think of was hurrying to a bus stop so I could get away from her. But the city buses were so crammed full of people that we didn't feel like getting on any of them.

The stores all sold cassette players, leather jackets, shampoo—stuff like that. We walked into yet another restaurant, a dumpling place, where everybody was eating standing up. We walked right out again, but as we did, she kept looking over her shoulder, back inside. Then there was another place, which had run out of everything but pig organs. She said she just couldn't remember where that one good restaurant was. We slipped into a wonton place and had a bowl apiece; I paid, of course. Then I asked her if she was taking the Number 3 bus or the Number 1. I figured if she took the 3, I'd take the 1. She said either would do. I said I wanted to go to the long-distance bus station to buy a ticket and asked her if she wanted to come along. Why I had to suggest that to her, I don't know. We went all the way through the night market again, through all the boiling and frying and clouds of steam, through all the people milling around and bumping into me. I had no idea, none, what the connection was between her and me or why we absolutely had to walk along here, getting shoved and elbowed, or if I really had to buy a long-distance bus ticket. When she saw me actually holding a bus ticket for early the next morning, she pointed to a shop next door selling southern-style foods and then pointed inside the place at some kind of soft, fluffy cake. I ignored her. Then we stood in a corner of this city where I didn't know a soul, waiting for the local bus to come. It came.

I managed to grab an empty seat for her. "Bye," I said when I got to my stop (which came before hers). She turned her face toward the window. I got off the bus but wasn't relieved at all. Nine-thirty in the Xi'an suburbs, walking through mud, suddenly I was hungry. As luck would have it, there ahead of me stood a place selling meat pastries and, incredibly, it was still open for business. I had a couple of the pastries (good ones, too) and washed them down with a bowl of hot sticky-dumpling soup. When I walked outside, I thought I saw the bus carrying Xiao Tong still coming toward me down the road, and I wondered whether I really *had* seen her.

"Next stop Xi'an—end of the line. One of our nation's renowned ancient cities, Xi'an has served as capital for more than ten dynasties over the long history of the Chinese people. . . ."

Xi'an.

The woman conductor had just yanked the woolen blanket out from underneath my pillow. I hopped down from the upper berth. Xi'an. No need for the woman on the PA system in that tiny one-and-a-half-square-meter booth (every time I went to the toilet, I saw her sitting there, right next door to the toilet) to make the announcement; from the train's deceleration, I already knew Xi'an was coming up. Just like all the other times I had shouldered my satchel and prepared to step into the press of disembarking passengers, I thought perhaps I ought to make some sort of parting remarks to the acquaintances I'd made on the trip. But I didn't. I did, however, make a rough calculation of my expenses since I'd started out just the day before: two box lunches, one beer, a cold plate of beef, and the noodles for breakfast. Altogether . . .

The comrades sent to greet me had the sign for the conference held high, so I spotted it from a good distance away.

I relaxed when I saw it. The first words spoken by the first comrade to shake my hand gave me a start: "Say, didn't you run into trouble on the way?"

What trouble? What was this all about? It seemed some-one had passed on word that my train had been delayed by a flash flood in the mountains, which is normally no big deal. This comrade, though, for some reason couldn't believe that I had managed to arrive in one piece. He gave me a good firm handshake but left me stuck with a grim thought: *somehow* I'd made it through safe and trouble free!

The conference was to open the following day, and we were going to drive out there bright and early in the morning. The plan, meanwhile, was to take the afternoon to do some sightseeing. I got a clear idea of the arrangements and checked my watch: still just a bit past ten in the morning. A van hauled us from the train station to the hostel, where we were to spend the night before heading off to Lu County and the conference. I went over to the check-in desk to make a phone call.

I gave her a call. Xiao Tong.

As soon as I began thinking of Xiao Tong, that summer three years ago drifted back into view. I was separated from my wife, feeling low and foul, as if she and I were involved in some sort of warfare. (I had no heart for fighting it out. We could have been happy together—if only, that is, I hadn't become what I am now.) It was in a gray fifties-era building that I had first met Xiao Tong. I was there with some journalist friends at a get-together called the Journalists' Trust, as we were all in the same line of work. But since each of us was either already divorced or in the process, it might have been better named the Singles' Club. I think it might have been I who came up with that Singles' Club tagline while proposing a toast. As for a good journalistic subheading to go with it, no one ever came up with anything. The opening speech was called "The Independent Woman." The speaker was Xiao Tong. She had recently got a divorce from a husband dead set against splitting up. Originally an athlete, she was powerfully built, proud, and bursting with an unreasoning drive to go out and take on her new life. (I have to admit that for me, it wasn't like that at the time.) She had prepared the lunch: fried sausages, ham, pickles, even cheese, and a ginger nut cake she had baked herself. And then that magnificent chicken. Even the way she carried it out to the table: unforgettable. She knew how to live and live well. The talk she gave, delivered in a strongly speculative vein, left a lasting impression, too. I remember only one phrase from it, when she said, "If a woman can love only one man, then she's not affirming the emotion of love but the man; only if a woman loves continually does she give affirmation to love in and of itself."

At the end of the get-together, our friends left Xiao Tong and me behind on our own; each one of them shook our hands as if wishing the two of us well in some unstated sort of way. I can't remember what she and I talked about then, except that she seemed to want me to stay for dinner (the get-together had been a lunch party), and I felt that wasn't really necessary. We met several times after that. She told me how she wrote compositions in English and how she spoke French in her sleep. She was the one who recommended that I read some of the world's most abstruse books. (I think I still have two that I bought after consulting the list she wrote out for me.) Later on, mutual friends were always filling me in on the latest about Xiao Tong: Xiao Tong's in love again, or Xiao Tong's gone through another breakup. The explanations of why she went to Xi'an conflicted. I tended to believe the one I could accept most readily: that she switched job assignments with a teacher who wanted to get back to her husband and child in Beijing. Then, of course, there were other factors in the background: after another frenetic breakup, Xiao Tong, in a huff, had stopped talking with her family.

This was where it stood when I arrived in Xi'an and gave her a call.

She would be happy to have me over for a visit but made it clear that she had nothing to offer me as her guest.

So after lunch at the hostel, I started out. The medical academy would be easy to find, I was given to understand, but even so I kept trying to talk myself out of going there right away: should I rush to get a quick look at the sights of Xi'an first, or should I spend the entire afternoon seeing Xiao Tong? Then again, we could take in the sights together. I decided on the latter.

Walking alongside a muddy road, at last I spotted the sign at the gate to the medical academy, and then I saw Xiao Tong.

A half month later, I'd finished the conference report and gone to see the terra-cotta soldiers, Empress Wu Zetian's Tomb, and the Tomb of the Yellow Emperor. Getting ready to leave on my return flight to Beijing, I wondered if perhaps I ought to make another trip to Wild Goose Pagoda or perhaps see Xiao Tong again. I decided on the former. No—I went to Xiao Tong's place first and then to Wild Goose Pagoda, because at her dormitory I saw a big padlock on the door. I knocked at the next-door neighbor's, but no one even knew who she was. When I said I'd been here a half month ago to see her, the neighbors suggested I go to the dean's office to check the personnel files. Check the files, or trust my memory? I decided on the latter.

When I got back to Beijing, would I tell my friends about Xiao Tong, or keep it to myself? I decided on the former. So I told a friend about what happened with Xiao Tong. He smiled. Xiao Tong had been back in Beijing for over three months, he said; he saw her almost every day. He could take me to her right away, too, since she was still around. Really? Terrific. It looked as if I'd really done a good turn—I'd deceived my own memory, or maybe my memory had deceived me. In any case, I didn't care to talk about it anymore. I started in telling my friend about my experience on the trip back from Xi'an, how I had had to stand up on the train for twelve hours straight.

He interrupted—which number train had I taken? "Number 126, of course." He smiled again, almost laughed this time: "Then you've come from Nanjing." He was right. I must have taken the plane back to Beijing!

But that sensation of standing on the train still lingered in my legs.

As soon as the train pulled up to the platform, I used my usual trick of flashing a journalist's ID and an interview-approval letter until I located the head conductor. To get a sleeper, you have to move in fast—you can't wait until after you've claimed a hard seat in third class. Unless you've made reservations four days ahead of time or waited five hours in line, this is the only chance there is to get some sleep on the trip. The head conductor very civilly led me to the dining-car corridor, pointed to a ten-centimeter-wide ledge along the wall, and said, "Sorry, but that's the best I can do—the sleepers are full. How about the third-class seats? . . ." I looked over and realized that I had no choice but to sit on the little ledge. The adjacent hard-seat car was impassable—this train was more of a city bus, what with people pressed up against one another so tightly that even turning around was impossible. The head conductor took me toward the door leading into the next car and, after making me promise three times not to let anyone into the dining car from the hard-seat section, let me have the spot. I promised and sat down. It felt like sitting on the rim of a toilet. I'd boarded the train at ten in the evening. It was due in Beijing at seven-thirty the following morning. For nine and a half hours, I would have to sit here, stuck in the position of someone taking a crap.

Half an hour after the train started moving, I went to see the head conductor again. He let me know that he'd already explained how things stood, that sleepers were out of the question that night, although something might be available tomorrow morning (which would be two hours before reaching Beijing). I said, "Then how about giving me a hard seat?" He said that would be more difficult than getting a sleeper. ("We can't pull someone out of his seat to make room for you. Take a look around, and if you see one, take it.") The third time I went to talk to the head conductor, he guided me out of the dining car, took his keys, and "clack," locked the dining-car door. I was left for good with the people standing in the hard-seat car.

It dawned on me that I was being held close by a mass of warm, sweaty bodies. All the connecting doors were open, allowing me to see straight to the back of the train, about a quarter of a mile away, people standing all the way to the end. We stood like horses, staring at one another, breathing into one another's faces. Next to us was a boiler room, so that with the dining-car door locked tight, the car I was in warmed up like one gigantic boiler. The windows were sealed shut, and there wasn't much air to begin with. At every stop, a few more people squeezed on, swelling the ranks of the standing passengers. No one was getting off the train. I had to grip the floor with my feet to keep myself upright, as there was only enough floor space for about half of either foot. I wondered how long I'd be able to keep this up.

A little over two hours into the ride, someone came up with the idea of getting off at the next station and waiting to get on the following train, which would probably be less crowded. Someone else said that was right, seeing as our train had left at ten at night and there wouldn't be anyone else getting on the trains after midnight. Sounded reasonable. But when a group of us climbed down onto the platform at the next stop and asked around, a short, fat platform attendant flatly advised that we get back on our own train. He couldn't guarantee we'd be better off on the later trains. In fact, he insisted that the next train through, the one we hoped to catch, would be even more crowded than this one. The only slight hope was a train coming out five hours later. "On the whole," he said with a wave of his hand, "you may as well stick with what you've got."

When we climbed onto the train again, the conductor asked why we were back. We told him what had happened. He immediately dismissed the platform attendant's remarks as a pack of lies. By then the train had been moving for ten minutes. Nothing left to do but check and recheck the time on my watch: six and a half hours to go, six and a quarter hours to go, six hours and fourteen minutes to go, six hours and thirteen minutes to go. . . . It reminded me of a long-distance bus trip I'd taken two years before in Henan . . .

I was sitting right behind the bus driver. Anytime a pig or chicken crossed the road or when we came up on a bicycle rider, he would blow the horn. The horns on those buses are as loud and harsh as they come. Every blast lasted about ten seconds, and then the sound rang in my ears for at least another fifteen seconds. Each time he hit it, I thought my heart was going to heave up out of my mouth. By a rough calculation, I figured that the two-hundred-mile trip would take around seven hours. With the driver blowing the horn about once every two minutes, that meant 210 horn blasts, each ten seconds long, plus the fifteen seconds of ringing in my ears. . . . But why go on? I thought. Ten minutes into the bus trip and my nerves were shattered. What would be left of me after half an hour? I realized I didn't care anymore—my ears had already hardened like iron . . .

In much the same way, I passed the nine and a half hours of that night numb to all feeling. The train didn't stop until seven in the morning. Just a half hour to go, but I felt sure I'd be able to stand for another nine and a half. Someone stuck his head out the window and reported that the train was temporarily held up.

"Clack." After being locked all night, the dining-car door opened. A conductor gave us an update: the train wouldn't be signaled into the station before ten-thirty. This meant that even though Beijing was only twenty-five minutes away, the train had to stay put for three more hours. No one's eyes registered any disappointment or anxiety, and no one said a word. The interior of the car was silence itself; everyone had to wait and endure. The connecting doors were locked—no one was allowed off the train even though all anyone had to do was walk to the nearest bus stop and catch a bus into the city . . .

It's a feeling I have, that even now I'm still on that train. My feet seem to be planted on the floor of that railway car, regardless of whether the train is stopped or moving, regardless of whether it's going anywhere at all. I have no way of telling this to my friends in Beijing—that I don't know when I'm ever going to arrive . . .

By that I mean I may have never been to Xi'an at all.

Translated by John A. Crespi

VACATION

Of the five on the trip, Robin and his Chinese girlfriend, who can't speak Chinese, make up one couple, Li and Annie the other. To help spread the costs of renting the car and cabin, they have taken along Tommy, Annie's teenage cousin. The drive out is rather unpleasant, and the driver, Robin, keeps making quick turns that pile the three in the back seat up into one another; twice at least he has swerved steeply to evade heavy trucks coming head-on. Li sits numbly, until his head again jounces against the ceiling of the car, and he hears Annie, her voice stern now, say, "Hey! You're not the only one in the car you know!" Unruffled, Robin makes a pretence of getting a more honest grip on the steering wheel. The mood in the car grows heavy, as if they were on the way to a funeral. Li moves quickly to fill the silence: "Actually, it wouldn't be so bad to die this way, seems to me." For that Annie presses the sole of her Birkenstock down on top of his foot, and keeps it there until they stop.

From Toronto it is two and a half hours to Lake George and its more than three thousand little islands, each with a cabin built to rent. Dusk is nearing by the time they get to the shore, where a flat-bottomed launch carries them to the islet. Along the way the launch bucks and heaves as if riding on a sea serpent's back.

Li has no idea what's eating at Robin. He was Annie's former classmate, and former admirer, but the rest of their history together is unknown to him. All he knows is that on the trip out Robin keeps talking about some sort of cave, a thirty-million-year-old, six-hundred-foot-deep cave. He still isn't clear on Robin's girlfriend's name (it's harder to remember than either a Western or Chinese name). Tommy sits in stubborn, stolid profile—seventeen years old, this little chunk of granite. The five of them are all staring off in at least three different directions. An imaginary scene pops into Li's head: Robin has seized the helm from the boatman and crashes straight into a rock, tumbling everyone off the boat and onto the shore like so many stage props.

Waves brush the banks all night as the island lays silent. Several times Li is on the verge of saying something to Annie, but fears his words will form the question: What are we doing here, with them? Annie has one knee inserted between Li's and an arm resting on his abdomen. No, no questions, because once it starts we'll run on all night. And that's hardly the point of taking a vacation, right?

Although he has never regretted it, Li has never had halcyon student days to think back on, and never in his life has he made progress under a teacher's guidance. At the job he holds now—Chinese instructor—he deals with his students kindly enough, so there's nothing really to reproach him with.

But for the very reason that this is a vacation, being roped in together with these relative strangers is all the more stupid. How would Annie answer his question?

"No, I totally disagree. They're not strangers at all. Which is all the more reason you should try to get to know them."

"Why?"

"Well, you have to face facts."

"I don't want to face facts!"

"Then you'll just have to accept the logic that the situation has advanced too far for simple denial to negate an accomplished fact."

Whenever Annie uses structurally complex declarative

sentences to demonstrate a point to Li, he feels that the English language is devastated by its own rationality. He wants to strike at the heart of Annie's argument with the perfect, succinct phrase, but finds himself at a loss. Not only that, debating is practically Annie's career. Just take a look at her CV: A Bachelor of Arts in French at Montreal, then a Master's in English at Vancouver; after that, during eight years of indecision over whether to pursue linguistics or English literature, she got a degree in sociology from Kingston and another in anthropology from Waterloo; then four years in Toronto, where she has only just graduated from law school and passed the bar examination, leaving her where she stands now—wavering over the decision to study for her first PhD or fourth MA. Her extended career as a student temporarily on hold, along comes this three-day trip to Lake George together with Li. So what will you do with your life when you're finished studying? Every time Li asks, Annie has a ready answer: I'll never be finished. Li interrupts, How old are you now? Annie asks back: What does age have to do with anything?

Li rolls over in bed counting the hairs around Annie's nipples and mulling over how much he hates picturing his girlfriend as the stereotypical North American female university student—smokes a little pot, listens to rock and jazz, eats health foods, rides a bicycle to the library with a load of books, her broad buttocks smothering the tiny little bicycle seat. . . .

Li lifts Annie's arm off his body and sets it down. He feels as lonely as ever, even with Annie, though he can't let it show because if he does, it will only get her started again. He picks up Annie's arm and sets it back on his abdomen.

It is nearly light before he gets to sleep.

Li pads, bleary-headed, to the toilet. Coming out of the bathroom, he realizes that the house is totally silent, and that there are bread crumbs all over the breakfast table. He goes into the kitchen and opens the refrigerator. It is the old-fashioned, bulbous kind, the kind that with its door open resembles a human body split apart, its internal organs ready to slither out. A cracked egg leaks yolk. Tommy is sitting alone in the living room, his hair dripping wet, facing out towards the bay.

"Good morning. Been swimming?"

No reply from the young man. Li tries another question.

"Where's everyone gone?"

"Out."

"Did they take the boat?"

No more response from the youth. What makes this kid so stubborn all the time?

"Could you tell me what time they'll be back?"

The youth shakes his head. Bemused, Li strides back into the bedroom, covers his head and sleeps. The pillow still holds Annie's scent, and her belt hangs, sword-like, straight down from a clothes hook. Li sees his mother gliding through the air above him.

Whenever he sleeps alone, Li sees his deceased mother in big cotton trousers gliding through the sky. He understands that she is searching for him, and that he is waiting, waiting for her to return to that old, sheepskin-covered rattan chair, head sagging, drooling, asleep. "Are you feeling better, Mother?" he asks, "Yes, yes, better than yesterday." His father lies in bed and yawns. He naps until three in the afternoon, and won't let his rest be interrupted by Mother before then. Sometimes Li wonders how the three of them made a family. They all accepted themselves as a family, that was all, and their forty years together developed an inertia that kept them from wanting to live any other way. A broad window lets in sunlight. From the distance come the cries of a peanut seller. A fire burns in the stove, heating a kettle of water. The old cat rests on Mother's big cotton trousers. Li buries his head against Mother's legs, calling: Meow, meow, kitty kitty. Mother is gone somewhere far, far away in her sleep, and all he can do is call, over and over: Meow, old kitty kitty, old kitty kitty. Li rolls over in bed and hears the rustle of his mother's gliding, like the sound of leaves rubbing against each other in an old, withered tree.

The weather is clear and bright under a wide and nearly cloudless sky. One by one, Li kills three mosquitoes that land on his shoulders, then goes outside. The Canadian flag, the red maple leaf, flutters in the breeze. Another flies on the island opposite. There are two ways to circumnavigate the island: one by traveling inland, pushing through the trees and underbrush;

the other by clambering over the boulders lining the shore and at times wading through water. Li chooses the latter because he fears withered trees, bleached and petrified like bones, as well as lichen and fungus with their stench of decay. These things remind him of something.

Back at the cabin after scrambling around the island, he smells a stink on his hands, the sort that would be left from burying many dead bodies. Tommy sits silently on a boulder in front of the cabin. Li waves at him with a pack of cigarettes. The young man shakes his head, and Li lights one for himself. In the distance across the vast lake people are visible. From time to time boats motor past, and sometimes people wave from them. It occurs to Li that until now he has only seen Tommy in profile.

Back inside the cabin, Li leafs through the books left there by the owner. Cookbooks, gardening manuals, fashion magazines, and children's readers. Li picks one at random and suddenly finds himself engrossed: A peaceful old farm village with pigs and sheep and silos and chickens. Two young hens dream of going off to a beautiful, beautiful place. So why not go? One night they slip away from the barn to discover new worlds. They rush off to the big city and strut proudly along the streets. They cut through a supermarket, where startled ladies and gentlemen stand aside to let them pass. They go to many marvelous places until at last in a fancy hotel a policeman catches them. They are hung upside-down by their feet on meat hooks in a big marketplace, and then a container truck takes them away to a chicken farm where they are stuck into little separate cages. Several times a day a worker in rubber boots pours out their feed and checks the air temperature. When the fat manager discovers they can't lay eggs, he sends them off with a batch of other "rejects" to a dark and gloomy slaughterhouse. The two hens run away and hide in an old abandoned mill, where thy huddle together and dream that an angel is feeding them grain from a golden scoop. They long for the peaceful old farm village. . . .

Li drops the book, rushes into the kitchen, and stuffs his mouth with two big handfuls of peanuts, feeling touched somehow by those two hens. The two hens have disturbed something inside of him. When Annie used to come over to his place, he'd unlock the front door and then hide himself, out on the balcony, behind a curtain, in a closet, and wait there until Annie found him. It was a game he used to play often as a child, after dinner, out for a stroll with his father. He remembered the intense delight of hiding behind a pile of cabbage on the streets of Beijing. The same magic thrill ran through him when Annie, gently chiding, was searching for him. He crawled out from under the bed and hugged her legs by surprise. He loved to see the startled expression on her face. They held each other for a long time, motionless. Annie stroked his head, and he looked up, "Mama, mama, mama." Annie looked down at him, enunciating clearly, "I am not your mama."

"Mama, mama," he went on. Again, Annie said, "I am not your mama."

"Mama," he continued.

Listen. I am not your mama. I might become your wife, but certainly not your mother."

"I've heard a lot of old men in the West call their wives mama."

"Look," Annie went on in a no-nonsense tone, "I'm not your mother."

"Why can't you use a little imagination?"

Li felt wounded somewhere inside.

"What does this have to do with imagination? I've never called you daddy."

"Because I don't want to be your daddy."

"It's best if nobody pretends to be anything."

"But that makes it easy for you, and I don't like it."

Li squirmed back and forth through Annie's legs.

"Be a little animal, Mama."

"I can be a little animal, but I won't be your mama."

Annie really makes Li want to cry. She is such a simple girl, so delicate from frenetic studying and a plain diet, her grasp of the world so narrow, her adherence to social conventions so total. She has her bath every evening and is up and onto the computer every morning, the alarm clock set unequivocally to six-thirty a.m. This is the Annie who, with her head buried between two pillows and one hand on the alarm clock, asked:

What right do you have to feel sorry for me?

"Oh, mama, mama." He gazed at her, wide-eyed and helpless.

"I'm not your mama."

"Why not give just a little, just for a while? Not even just for a little while?"

"No. I told you already, I'm not your mama."

Li crawled on the floor, not wanting to believe in Annie's blandness.

Li takes a bottle of beer outside the cabin, still thinking how through the hot, muggy night he punished Annie with silence. Annie lay facing the wall. He had shifted over to the far edge of the bed and was tracing figures on the floor with his finger. When they made up after a fight, Annie could just do it, no reason needed. He needed a reason. But what was it? It wouldn't come to him. All he could do was ask, over and over, Why can't you see it, Why can't you? She just couldn't. He wanted her to see her own predicament. Your life is like a war, do you know that? She agreed to that completely, so what was the use in saying it? She's just incapable, incapable of changing anything. Annie, you're a practical-minded girl, you can take on any good, solid task that comes your way. But what does your life really amount to? Have you thought about it once, even once?! Annie has no desire at all to meddle with his understanding of her—what could it have to do with her? Annie, listen, we're each other's front lines. Sure, no question about it. Better to say nothing, hold it all back, let this stifling summer night smother me. He massages his abdomen. This suffocation has somehow made him fatter, or maybe it's just gas, because when he looks in the morning, it's gone.

Still no sign of Annie and the others. The lake lies wide and calm as ever, but it is a lifeless calm, the calm of vacation. Tommy sits alone looking out at these other lives. Li has an urge to tousle the young man's hair, but his nerve fails him. If he were a horse or a big dog, it would be different.

The boat circles around from the back of the island. Li raises his beer bottle to the passengers.

"Sorry, Li, but I didn't want to wake you." Li is glad to see Annie in high spirits. "We went to a little market on the opposite shore. . . . Sorry?" Li asks her what general direction it was in. "Oh, it's complicated, you go around the island across the way . . . no, around a whole lot of islands. Nothing worth seeing. Some people selling paintings and sculpture. We met a Russian girl called Lyuba, from Chernobyl. Just turned thirteen. I talked some Russian with her."

"The Glorious Fatherland, the Glorious Capital, the Glorious Land of Socialism."

Li loudly recites the Russian he learned in middle school. Robin and his Chinese girlfriend look on gleefully, but aren't interested in talking to Li. Li thinks he might ask Robin where that cave is located.

"Too bad, though. Lyuba can only stay on Lake George until Saturday. She has to go back. Some very nice Canadians paid the money for her to come. We all wish that she could stay a while longer, and we're worried about her future. Hey, look at that." A small snake is lying across a rock. Annie's reaction is the same as when she feeds the pigeons in Toronto.

"Don't move. It might be poisonous."

"That's right. There are only two kinds of snakes on the island, poisonous and non-poisonous." This comment from Annie infuriates Li. Tommy darts in front of Li and deftly catches the snake by the head.

Robin comes up to them, his girlfriend beside him, her arm around his waist. "Having fun?" "Great fun." Annie puts her arm around Li. The four of them stand in a face-off, as if ready to begin a square dance, or burst into laughter. The teenager wraps the snake around his neck.

Annie has sunblock on now, but probably put it on too late—her skin is as red as if she'd been stung all over by hornets. Still she insists on sunning herself. Li looks again at Robin's girlfriend. She was born in Toronto, but her distant place of origin shows through in that clinging and manipulative way she has. Li lies back on a rock and finishes two bottles of beer. He feels enervated. By the time the alcohol has begun to wear off, the others have swum out to a massive rock out in the lake. Annie is there, waving to him to come over.

Looking up from its base, the rock appears quite tall. But looking down from its top you can see that it's barely fifteen meters high. Annie comes up from behind and hugs Li around the stomach.

"Cheese belly." Li wants to pat his belly, but Annie won't let him. "Cheese, beer, and gripes."

"Easy now." Annie covers Li's mouth with her hand, afraid he'll say, "I'm getting old."

Robin and his girlfriend help one another climb down the rear face of the rock. Tommy, chest out and holding his breath, stands at the rock's edge. His body is well muscled, his hair tied back in a small ponytail, and his toes grip the rock so firmly they seem nearly to sink in. Li has seen fine-looking young men like Tommy in many places, at figure-skating competitions, for instance. Li cocks his head to look down at the water, a little mistrustful of the lake's depth, and noting that the leap outward will have to clear more than two meters to avoid the boulders below. The young man leaps with precise control, arms spread, chest forward, head back, legs straight and taut; in less than two seconds Li's entire youth flashes past—he too has dived like this.

The young man bursts from the water and shakes back his hair in a supremely winning way. He smiles, directly at Li, it has to be at Li, and Li understands what is required of him. But his feet won't budge an inch. He feels he has reached an age that allows him to comfortably decline a challenge, to wave it off with no sense of shame. He descends along the rear face of the rock. The wind is blowing at him face-on, and in the distance he sees trees bending and heaving from the gusts. The clouds too move drunkenly. Normally Li can see hundreds of spectacular shapes and visions in the clouds; now all he sees are drifting, cottony giants with contorted eyes and twisted mouths. Li suddenly senses Annie near him, still there with him in the world, here on this rock.

"Why don't we leave Toronto, go to a small village in Ontario and get down to making forty babies. Thinking about it, sitting here on this rock, it sounds like the most natural thing in the world."

Annie isn't giving serious attention to his heartfelt words. She just leans close into him.

"That was great, champ." Annie turns, "Let me give you a kiss."

The young man climbs up on the rock. With an emotionless sweep of the hand he brushes Annie's arm from his shoulders. Annie replaces her arm. He brushes it away again, adjusts his ponytail and the amulet over his chest, and leaps away into the air. This time when he surfaces he doesn't wave to Li.

"As you've probably already guessed, we have a little bastard on our hands. What can you do with someone Tommy's age? He never says anything, and always has that stubborn look on his face. He does know how to dive, though."

"Uh-huh. I need a cigarette."

As the sun descends a vague coolness comes into the air. They decide to take the rowboat out. Li watches as the others go about competently gathering up fishing tackle, oars, a sail, and surfboards, and put on life vests. The last to get in the boat, Li sits in the stern. They cast off and row out into the tranquil lake. The water spreads into the infinite distance and waves slap the shoreline with the sound of the sea. No one on the boat looks like they're enjoying themselves, however.

After dinner the five of them sit in a circle of wicker chairs, no television, telephone, or electric lights; just a pair of candles to gather around as fatigue from the day's outdoor activities affects them to varying degrees. The hour is still too early for bed, but slapping mosquitoes while listening to the waves grows tedious quickly. Li reaches for a magazine. On the first page is a photograph of a young girl, with a caption below that goes, "Dearest Karen, It's been three weeks, but my eyes are still red and swollen. Still I keep asking myself, Why didn't I get in the car with you on that day? I'll never forget how sad that car looked. Karen, I'll never have a better friend than you. Karen, I love you." After reading this letter from a girl to her friend killed in a car accident, Li notices a word that keeps reappearing in the magazine. He asks Annie what a "teenager" is. A young person between thirteen and seventeen years old, she replies. Robin adds that Canada has approximately five million teenagers. His girlfriend corrects him: Was it five million or nine million? I remember that five thousand teenagers commit suicide a year, or was it nine thousand? The discussion turns to the teen magazine, and closes with the conclusion: God himself can't understand teenagers.

Listening to the talk, Li feels himself of an age where birth and death are both far away. Tonight he wants to be in bed face to face with Annie, again with her arm resting in that hopeless way on his abdomen, her, asleep, while he lies awake without the strength either to get up and go read in the kitchen, or to get himself to sleep right away. He is at the age where getting to sleep is harder than waking. What he used to do was shake Annie awake, but when she realized he wanted only to slip into her arms like a child, she would fall heavily and hopelessly back to sleep. It was a shameless thing for him to do, and he knew it.

"Good night." "Good night."

Robin and partner stand up. Tommy has long since disappeared. Li goes with Annie into the bedroom. Immediately he feels that uncomfortable wetness. As always, he knows only too well that this is only urine, and that he's going to wet himself again and again. He goes into the bathroom, wipes himself dry with toilet paper, and returns to see Annie waiting for him watchfully. He wets himself again. He lays face downward on the bed, stretching one leg in between Annie's legs and resting it on the bed sheet. Annie is waiting for something, but he's not sure what. Annie lifts her buttocks to adjust her nightgown; he is still losing urine in tiny spasms. He clamps down on Annie's heel with his own to try and stem the flow, but it only comes faster. He recalls how most of the time he is so unusually dry, like the pebbles a young boy plays with for so long and then clamps between his knees. Annie shuts her eyes and presses close to him, as if readying herself for some sort of therapy. He strains to concentrate, but wets himself again so that now he absolutely has to wipe himself dry once more. He slips hastily out of bed, hearing Annie release a sigh behind him.

"I'll be right back."

Facing the bathroom mirror he notices how harsh and fierce he looks, and shivers violently, as if gripped by Death itself. He is afraid of wetting himself again when he gets back in bed, but fears even more that Annie might already be asleep. Staring at the face in the mirror, he can't remember when this shameful thing started. He sits resignedly down on the toilet until his legs go numb before finally getting up and lurching into the kitchen.

He opens a beer, wondering in the cruel summer night if he matters to anyone, to Annie, to those less close to him, or to those who have died. He drinks down the entire bottle in one breath and opens another; he doesn't drink for pleasure, he drinks to be drunk, drinks because he's at the age of summing up what he is. He affirms that thought, opens another bottle, and carries it outside.

Ah, the lake, it makes him want to burst into song—Four hundred years ago the Indians here dwelt. The Indians here dwelt. . . . He can't think of a line to follow that one. A shadow starts in the darkness—Tommy, gazing at the sky. He speaks at length, but rapidly and vaguely, apparently about something happening in the sky, something like a star leaving its path. Li looks up, too, and as he does Tommy goes back indoors. The lake slaps at the shore, though there is no wind over the water. The waves arrive from far, far off, from the wake of a passing ship, coming perhaps from the United States.

"Sorry to make you wait so long. When are we going to go and find that cave?" It's nearly noon by the time Li comes out into the living room where the other four have gathered to decide what to do. Li remembers last night's plan of going to the cave Robin had spoken of. According to Robin, the cave was a truly magical place.

"Sorry, Li." Somehow Li can't ever fix Robin's face in his memory.

"We've broken our promise. Sorry about that, really. We have to go back to Toronto today."

"You mean now?"

"No. We'll have lunch first."

Li glances at Annie. First your old schoolmate here ropes us into coming to the island; now he wants to pack us all back to Toronto. Avoiding his gaze, Annie turns to look out over the lake. Li keeps glaring at her. It's because he wants to save money on the car, did you catch that? To save money on the car, he wants to go back, and we have to go back, too. Who got us into renting a car together with them anyway?

Robin and his girlfriend go to their room to pack, where they continue their spat in hushed voices. Li too begins rehearsing to himself the all-night argument he will have with Annie the coming evening in Toronto. Thinking about it upsets him: first there will be a barrage of interrogation, followed by some thoughtful mature deliberation, and then he'll hit home with that one perfect phrase. He wants to come up with that phrase now. When the ferry has left the small island, he recalls how on that same island an author had once had a magical night of writing: by the light of two candles, in a deep stillness disturbed only by soft breezes passing through the room, he wrote as if possessed. . . .

Back on the mainland Robin pulls the car keys from his pocket, but is stopped from getting to the car by Annie.

"If you insist on driving, the rest of us are walking back to Toronto."

Both Annie's and Tommy's hands stretch out. Robin tosses the keys to Tommy, and Annie and Li get into the back seat. The car winds along the wooded lakeshore and past tastefully designed vacation cottages half hidden in the trees. On Fridays the wealthy of Toronto drive to the lakeshore, hop into private powerboats and motor off to private islands for three-day stays. After that it's back to the city through the Sunday evening traffic.

Tommy pulls over near a tall slope, gets out of the car and runs uphill, shedding clothes as he goes. The cold war going on in the car is just peaking. Robin keeps turning around to face the back, "Listen, Annie. Let me talk, Annie." "I don't want to hear it." Robin is angry, his girlfriend is too, and Li decides to stay out of it—he argues with Annie and no one else. All he wants is to get to Toronto as soon as possible. At the top of the slope Tommy is wearing just a bathing suit as he stands erect, holds his breath, spreads his arms and leaps. Robin is motioning with his arms over the seatback for emphasis, and his girlfriend and Annie are slapping his arms back and forth. Robin gets out of the car and runs. The three left in the car are breathing heavily in anger as they watch him charge up to the crest of the slope and stare down over the edge. When he begins gesticulating at them wildly, Li recovers himself: Robin has found the cave, the six-hundred-foot deep cave.

At the base of the cliff a wide field studded with rocks extends for a full fifty meters before meeting lovely Lake George. Li forces himself to look far away, into the sky, his mind filled with the words he wants to say to Annie. But every time he opens his mouth, Annie's fingernails bite into the palm of his hand.

Translated by John A. Crespi and revised by
Gregory B. Lee and Daniel Wang

GOING HOME

In the north of England, seventy miles past Scarborough, there is a small coastal town called Wearmouth. For nine hundred years all the townspeople have been buried in its cemetery. At the far end of the cemetery stands a cottage. That is where I live.

I am old now. My eyes have long since grown accustomed to the gray skies and the green pastures, the wet winds and dim light of England. At this age, whether I am a farmer or a writer does not matter much, but whether I am a cemetery attendant or a gardener does. The people in the town would never agree to someone outside their religion caring for their graves, and naturally would not allow such a person to be buried among them.

I am quite content to be a cemetery gardener, and often stroll over the fields, which I like to watch closely, particularly at harvest time. Surely it is because I walk with my hands behind my back that I can hear the shouts of children carried on the wind. "Good morning, Li." "Good evening, Li." I feel no need to turn and respond. I simply bow affectionately in the direction of the fields, narrowing my eyes to watch the fierce wind plundering the waves of wheat and see the church steeple concealed deep in the fields. Every time the harvest season arrives I murmur to myself that the Chinese people's god is not in the church, but in the fields.

Many years have passed, and whether or not I speak with the people in the town is no longer important. They and I have grown old in an unchanging relationship. The children of the adults who used to call me Li still call me that. Sometimes when they come to pay their respects to their buried parents, I stand with them for a while.

Like the country cemetery and the church, my reason for being here has long been forgotten, or rather, the meaning behind it all has long since been lost. I look after the greenery through all four seasons, and as long as it doesn't rain, I go into the fields to look at the sky. I do not go out if the rain is light, but must if it storms. When the rain is heavy I sit on the long bench in front of the church, opposite the small square, holding a red umbrella. At such times, when I look into the shop windows, people are likely saying, "There you go, the Chinese bloke is waiting again."

Quite right. I am waiting.

I was waiting for the arrival of someone else from China. A young person, I was sure of that, possibly with a rucksack, who after leaving the bus station and turning the corner by the second-hand bookshop, will walk straight into the small town square. There he will see me in the rain, and will come over to listen to my story. If he wants to listen, I will be able to depart this world, or as Chinese people put it, I can go home.

The long night seemed to be rattling on about a last will and testament. In the morning when I awoke, the sky was overcast. The sound of thunder could be heard far in the distance. I got up as soon as I heard the first raindrops on the gravestones.

But while putting on my raincoat I sent my hand through the underarm seam and inside the lining three times in a row, and when I closed the door behind me, I felt as if part of my body was caught on something, as if I had sprouted a tail. A few steps out the door and I was struck, but not altogether surprised, to spot two newly dug graves side by side. Then an old woman came up and greeted me. "So glad to see you." She seemed to be driving at something. I couldn't help but turn to face her. Her fat, rubbery legs seemed to convey an invitation of some sort.

The rain let up as I sat on the bench in the small square at the center of town. There was no one around, only the sound of the church bell—was everyone off getting buried?

It occurred to me that I had encountered something odd like this once before.

It was back when I was a student in London. Looking to get out of the city to relieve my boredom, I headed straight into Wearmouth. Leaving the bus station, I found myself in this small square. That was before they had set up a tourist shop that sells plastic dildos. One after another cottages appeared, as if from a dream; small bundles of newspapers, still waiting to be picked up, lay on every doorstep. Not a soul was in sight, just like today. All I could see were plump horses in the distance, seeming half submerged in the green, sloping pastures. By the time I reached the breakwater, the beach was full of people—probably the entire town was there. They were evenly dispersed over the beach, facing the sea at dusk. There was no disturbance on the water, and nothing out of the ordinary seemed to be taking place. The hands of some of the old gentlemen nervously twitched, shaking their dogs' leads, but the dogs had gone elsewhere. The children uttered not a sound. These gentlemen and their wives, old and young, hair all smoothly combed, standing so solemnly and respectfully, were all looking at something that I could not see. There was something stirring in their hearts, and their silence had some larger meaning. It was as if some tacit gesture was all that was needed for them to go down to the sea together. I did not know what they were waiting for, but I knew that they had their reason to wait, while I did not.

I was already middle-aged by the time I came to London,

but all the same, every day on the way to and from school, book bag over my shoulder, I swung my arms about as if a teenager inside me was pointing to this and that. Near Paddington Station stood a cluster of chimneys, and the gray houses enclosing the square at King's Cross reminded me of a coal yard in Beijing near Xizhimenwai. Against the backdrop of Hyde Park at dusk, the basin in front of the abattoir on Ox Street, where the mullahs used to wash their hands before slaughtering the livestock, floated clearly into sight; sometimes, before the entrance to the Imperial Bank of Commerce in Piccadilly Circus, the door of the Beijing grain shop tucked in a corner of Jinshifang Street flashed up, or it could have been the vehicle repair shop at Gongmenkouwai, or a crowd of people queuing for registration stubs outside the dental hospital in Xisi. Down a narrow alleyway in Euston I even saw a white horse flash past Guanganmenwai.

London's past rumbled into the distance behind the cars of the Underground. I used to ride in those linked metal coffins, and on occasion would encounter a Chinese person. Invariably, after a quick glance at one another, we would turn away. Then intentionally or otherwise, we would look at one another again, our eyes sending an unambiguous message: what the hell are you doing here? All right, and what the hell about you?

That is why I left London for Wearmouth.

And that is why I cannot forget the strange day when the people of Wearmouth went to look at the sea, as if they thought it was about to leave them, and had to send it on its way.

The church bells continued to ring, the music of the hymns and the pipe organ rose and fell. So today was Sunday and everyone was at church. But what was that old woman doing in the cemetery by herself? As I was thinking about this the tall doors of the church opened and old couple after old couple walked down the stone steps supporting each other. Someone doffed his hat, nodded to me, and said "Happy Easter."

So today was Easter Sunday.

The priest and deacon also came out, followed by a group of chubby altar boys in their vestments, all of them making gestures of blessing to the crowd of people, and to me. The church doors then closed again. Everyone dispersed from Mass to have their splendid family suppers of roast pork or fried chicken. Everyone had been given a colored egg. Perhaps some would dress up as Easter bunnies and parade in the street, so that whoever met up with one of them would have good luck. Facing the closed-up church and shops, and the street, silent now again, I sat alone. Absentmindedly, I uttered a Chinese word: porridge.

Any way I thought about it, no matter how I tried to get around it, today that word meant just one thing to me: Mother. It made me weep. The tears of old men and children are the same: once they come there is no stopping them. In that sense, their tears are much like those of any poet.

As I wiped my tears I went on thinking—every cloud that floats away carries with it some event of the past. The old woman had chosen the day of Jesus's return to visit the cemetery; it meant she understood resurrection.

In fact, when she was young, she used to love coming to the cemetery, and from a distance would watch me tending the greenery. Sometimes she would greet me, sometimes not, and when she did not, she would stay a bit longer. She loved taking her shoes off and going barefoot, thinking her private thoughts as she wandered around. I never knew how to say her name properly—Maria, Julia, Moira. But I was young then, and liked to call her name. When I saw that far-off look in her eyes, I called to her less. There was just that once, when she came up and pressed her cheek against mine. Just as it occurred to me how pleasant it would be to wrap my legs around hers, she extricated herself. Or did she?

Maria had been a maid. Her employer was named Smith. Mr. Smith liked to wear Scottish tweed jackets, and he also liked to converse with me, sometimes at length. He had long had a problem with his throat, so Maria's main task was to help him to talk, to translate his guttural sounds into, "Hello, I have lived enough and really would like to leave this world, but I should not be hasty, you Chinese people understand this." Or it was, "I haven't lived enough. Lived enough? That's a Chinese way of thinking."

It was probably because Maria liked to come alone to the cemetery that I could sometimes hear strange things in Mr. Smith's gurgling voice, things like, "So you have had a good time then?" Eventually it got to where I was sure I could understand him, so I would gurgle back, "So you have had a good time then?" And he would energetically nod his head.

Mr. Smith has been lying in his grave for many years now. Maria opened an antique shop selling furniture, glassware, crockery, hanging clocks, floor lamps, mirrors . . . all from the Victorian period. She had thousands of objects all piled up in her shop, probably left to her by Mr. Smith. Sometimes I went in with the idea of asking whether she had a coffin. But I was afraid of giving her a fright. She opened her doors every day, not to make money, any more than I went in to spend money. Old Maria wore bifocals, and as soon as she saw me come in, she would pretend to be reading a book. She first read from left to right, and then from right to left, and finally from top to bottom. That was because when she was young, in a pub in London, she once saw three people sitting down and reading, one was English, another Jewish and the third was Chinese.

There are no other Chinese people in Wearmouth apart from me, so naturally there are no Chinese bookshops. There is only a sign opposite Maria's antique shop with the Chinese characters for Phoenix Restaurant. The first time I went to the restaurant I was very happy, but when I asked whether it was Sichuanese or Cantonese food, the owner waved his hand at me, so I asked if it was a Chinese restaurant, and again the owner simply waved his hand at me. I realized that what he meant was, "Don't ask." So I simply sat there for a while without ordering food or asking for tea, but I left a tip, simply to see a painting hanging on the wall. "Is it painted by a Chinese person?" The owner waved his hand. "It's not by a Chinese?" The owner waved his hand again. "Let's speak English then."

He continued to wave his hand, waving through many. In my old age, when I come again to look at the painting, the owner is no longer around. When I, too, am gone, that painting will still be there.

It is an oil painting, a Chinese palace standing on the slope of a jade-green mountain, with a decorated archway in the foreground and a pavilion in the distance. That is all—I mean, there are no people. It is a fine spring day in the painting, and the landscape is rich and luxuriant. The scene is brightly lit but you cannot see the sun, nor is there any indication of the period depicted, just a sense of magnificent structure with no reference to historical cycles of rise and fall. I never tire of looking at it, this gift from heaven, rich with the authenticity and warmth of a grand continent—it is something that a people long accustomed to gazing at the sea will never be able to understand.

Every time I leave the Phoenix Restaurant is like leaving a clinic that treats anxiety. The light in the painting is so soft, like music, or like the Chinese language. The last time I heard people talking Mandarin was on the London Underground:

"Or we could simply go back. Why don't we just go back?"

"Who said we shouldn't go back? Can we get back? If I were Ma Yo-Yo I would go back."

"He's called Yo-Yo Ma."

"I don't care which Ma he is, they give him three thousand pounds just for taking a pee!"

Mentioning this conversation makes me think of another story.

DUO DUO

The small zoo at Wearmouth is filled with lions, tigers, elephants, and whales, but they are all painted stone sculptures. The little kids under five like to point at them excitedly. There are also seven or eight crocodiles that spend the entire day sleeping coiled up in a heap. Seeing their jagged teeth makes me think of the watermelon seeds spilled on the ground along the crooked streets of London's Chinatown. Often a child's question would interrupt my meditations:

"How come they are so ugly?"

"They're just very old," the parents would reply.

The older I become, the more I like to look at them, sometimes for a good part of the day. I never tire of watching them because that radar antenna on my forehead no longer needs to turn. I particularly like to watch one crocodile imprisoned on its own. It looks just like the others, but if that were so, why does it need to be isolated? Many years ago I thought of asking the keeper, but by chance I happened to hear him talking with someone else, which made me give up my idea of bringing up the matter.

"That Chinese guy is a bit odd."

"I agree," said the keeper. "He's sneaky . . ."

"What do you mean?"

"It's nothing much. He just has this sneaky way of . . ."

I listened, sneakily, and, sneakily, they kept talking.

"It's nothing, really. It's just that he sneakily picked his nose a couple of times . . ."

The two of them chuckled, sneakily.

Their laughter was so like the sound of rain. I shouted in

98

my own ears: It's raining! It's raining! But when I opened my eyes, there was no rain. Dusk had fallen. I was still sitting on the bench.

It would happen all the time. I would gradually doze off, then wake with a start when I heard the rain falling—Quick! The window's still open, the clothes are still outside on the line. It was only when I had calmed myself down that I remembered, yes, there was an open window, the one from which you could see all the way to White Pagoda Temple, that there were clothes still hung out to dry, and that the clothesline was still strung over to Old Mrs. Shi's place at No. 35A. Every time this happened I would become paralyzed with fright and would have to find someone to talk with as soon as possible. Maybe that is why I mutter to myself, or when I feel the urge, go to the zoo to see the old crocodile.

There was one other time when I could no longer bear it, because of two leather shoes that would not stop fluttering before my eyes. Two shoes with worn down heels stumbling along the sidewalk. The tighter I shut my eyes, the more vigorously they moved along, until I finally realized that several years before on a street in Chinatown I had seen a shoe tread on a clot of phlegm and go six steps before it completely rubbed off. I didn't want to see that shoe anymore, so I slipped out of the cemetery on to the road. In the distance I heard someone saying in foreign-accented Chinese, ". . . I love you . . . I love you . . . ." I looked carefully to see who it was. A fair-haired girl was speaking to herself as she walked along, head bowed, as if carrying something on her back. "I love you, you fuck me, I love you, you fuck me." Who had taught her this? Intrigued, I forgot about that pair of shoes . . . .

Yet I still heard something moving, echoing. I had not been dreaming, or so I thought, because in England I never had dreams. It was as if dream stood in for logic, for something I could not have dreamed.

I finally realized what that sound was—a milkman's pushcart rumbling along the cobbled road in the distance—and understood that I had slept through Easter on the bench. It was already light. I had not had any pleasant dreams, but did hear a voice greeting me.

"Good morning, young man. How come you're lying here? Aren't you worried that I'll steal your wife?"

The milkman came up to me. Was I on this bench waiting for a Chinese boy, or was the boy waiting for an old Chinese man? The milkman did a little two-fingered salute at the peak of his cap, and pushed his cart on. He saw that I did not want to share the joke with him.

I have not liked jokes for a long time, and anyway, with English jokes, I always want to laugh when I don't understand them, and never laugh when I do. For example, a life insurance salesman. The first thing he said when he came in was, "If you die we will pay you one-hundred thousand." I was just at the point of waving him away when he came back with, "Dismembered arm, thirty thousand." I got up, but before I had taken a step, he spouted, "Leg, fifty thousand." I opened the door and pointed outside, but before I maganged to speak he was already saying, "Loss of a kidney, vision, voice—compensation guaranteed!"

I walked through the small town toward the cemetery. The sky was overcast but it was brighter than on a clear day. It was impossible to open your eyes, so bright you could not tell whether it was morning or evening, winter or summer. I pulled myself together, and spotted the keeper, eyes squinting in a smile, standing at the entrance to the zoo.

"Good morning, young man. Have you come to look at the sea?"

I stopped. "I've seen enough of the sea. I've come to look at the crocodile."

Every time I visit the zoo, the keeper is always there with his hand digging around in his trouser pocket. "Good morning, sir," I say to him, and he begins to dig around in his pocket, waiting until he gets his hand out before replying. Every time he pulls out a long string of keys, which he hangs on a wooden peg that looks like a penis, or the handle for flushing the lavatory.

"Here to see the crocodile?" The keeper seemed to make some sort of connection. "An old Chinese fellow has been coming here every day for forty years."

"Forty years? More like seventy years."

"It's quite something. Chinese people always like to look at the crocodile."

"There have been crocodiles in China for a long, long time, so Chinese people have seen enough of them, but England hasn't got any, so they enjoy seeing them."

The keeper shrugged. "Well, have a nice visit."

"Thanks."

Every time I sit cross-legged on the ground to face the old crocodile, it is as if I am facing a cemetery.

The cemetery is too quiet. Even when there are children playing around, it is still too quiet. Let me go on living, and go on forgetting. Let the days pass with nothing to hold them back. Looking at the cemetery I felt at ease. I always take good care of it. The grass is always exceptionally lush. A few horses cross over from the hillside pasture to amble aimlessly about.

"Okay, go home now," I call to them. "You've been playing around here enough now, so go home, this is no place for you to be fooling about."

They are quite intelligent. Even though they are big and tall, love galloping and gnawing on tree bark, as soon as they hear me calling, they slowly move on. But there is one horse which gallops wildly up and down the cemetery grounds, so that I have to shout to it separately, "Okay, Young Four, I see that you can run, but it's time to go home."

He is disobedient, and sometimes comes rushing toward me, head down as if he wants to butt me. I know that he won't really, that when he reaches me he will turn his head and run off again. I call him Young Four because he looks so young. I reserved Young Seven and Young Eight for the two crocodiles that are always squashed under the other big ones. The old one that is shut up on its own I called Third Master.

Every time I sit cross-legged on the ground, the keeper tact-fully moves to one side, or simply steps over to the entranceway to have a cigarette. But today for some reason he hung about beside me. "May I trouble you a minute? I'm curious about something."

"No trouble at all."

"You haven't noticed any change in him?" He points to Third Master.

When I realized that someone who was incapable of making a joke was trying to make a joke, I felt utterly drained.

"What I mean is, you don't think he's dead, or fake, do you?" I didn't answer. "No? Because it has occurred to me, to me, even, that I haven't seen any change in him for several decades. No one has ever paid him any mind, except for one girl who wanted to get a closer look. She poked her head in through the bars. It's too bad I wasn't around at the time. Her scarf was too long, and it hung down—luckily she hadn't knotted it."

"And then what happened?"

"What happened? Nothing happened." The keeper put his hands in his pockets. "The girl still works as a typist in the BBC block that a Japanese company bought up. The scarf must still be in his stomach. She was Japanese, you know." A bit self-importantly, he stepped off to one side.

The keeper had been quite fat when he was young, though his bottom looked overly compact, as if he was deliberately holding it in. Now he is old, and his bottom has flattened out, but his eyes are still mirthless and his lips are as thin as ever, thin as the rim of an unused condom.

Third Master's drab brown eyes were as small as wasps, and his cumbersome body made me think of the wooden shoes people wore in ancient China. I waved my hand in front of his eyes.

"Five pounds." The keeper came at me gesturing like he was going to fine me, then began fumbling around in his pocket until he drew out a handful of coins, which he poured into Third Master's big maw.

Third Master remained motionless, not even salivating. With his mouth full of money he looked rather cunning.

"I'm sorry, I was only doing what that old man used to do." The keeper spoke with great self-assurance. "He's done this on at least one occasion. In my opinion, the old man came to see the crocodile as a sort of experiment, as if he wanted to prove something. He also talked to him, for a long time at a stretch. There seemed to be some kind of debt between them. To tell you the truth, he hoped the croc would up and die. I really don't understand it, but it reminds me of a story. . . ."

"I *am* a story, would you like to hear it?"

"The story goes like this. An English gentleman was traveling in China and took his dog into a restaurant. The waiter asked him what he wanted to eat, and the gentleman asked what could be done regarding his dog. The waiter replied, "Glad to be of service," and went off with the little dog. It was a pedigreed husky, snow white all over, and with an equally beautiful name, Bianca. . . ."

". . . which was also the name of the dish," I interrupted.

"There's another story that I reckon you definitely won't have heard.

Do Chinese people celebrate Christmas, or that other festival—that big one in China?"

"Spring Festival."

"That's right, Spring Festival. England has a holiday called Valentine's Day, and one year it happened to be on the very same day as Spring Festival. That old Chinese fellow invented a kind of Chinese hamburger, a sausage wrapped up in something like a rice flour bun—and he walked along the street holding a basket of these things shouting, 'Today is a Chinese holiday. Try a Chinese hamburger.' The people of the small town all politely declined; only one young woman exchanged words with him. 'So, Valentine's Day is China's biggest festival?' In a split second something happened to the old man. First he seemed dumbstruck, and then he did something unspeakable. He savagely bit off one end of the Chinese hamburger and squeezed the sausage out of the bun, cackling obscenely at the young woman the whole time. And that wasn't the end of it. He spent that whole night shouting and wailing in the graveyard, terrifying everyone in the vicinity. Afterwards he denied it completely, claiming that it was just some ghosts howling, and that squeezing the burger was something he had learned from British students and not a Chinese tradition at all."

"That was serious," I sighed.

"Even more serious than that," the zookeeper said, moving

his face closer to mine. "The old Chinese man had been coming to see the crocodile every day for years until both he and it had grown old. One day, just like every other day, I stepped out for a cigarette and returned to find the old man missing. He hadn't left by the front entrance, I can tell you that."

"You mean, it ate him?"

"I didn't say that. I only said that he went missing."

"You're lying."

"No one in this town has lied for nine hundred years."

The keeper's face seemed younger somehow.

"You might not believe it, but I'm not lying," he continued earnestly. "Anyway, the old gentleman disappeared and the crocodile hasn't taken a shit since."

At that he turned his head so as to prevent me from seeing whether or not he was smiling. I guessed that he was giggling, for the few coins remaining in his trouser pockets were rattling. "Would you excuse me?" He went out, leaving me with the story of the old Chinese man.

After several decades of not saying anything to one another, this fellow had gone and set me up as part of a story. This was unacceptable. You people can't bury me like that. I heard a voice ringing incessantly in my ears, sending me into a panic. This was unacceptable. Unacceptable. I struggled to stand up, ducked low and slipped into the enclosure. I had to retell this story my way.

I stomped back and forth over the length of Third Master, retracing that damned old man's life over and again until

I had crushed it into a pile of powder as white as cocaine. I say "stomp," but "wade" is more accurate. It had become dry as powder. If I had not done this the crocodile would still be a crocodile with an old Chinese man and a Japanese scarf in its belly and a big handful of English pennies in its mouth. It was gone. The only one inside the enclosure was me. The old Chinese man was also gone, leaving just me inside a story about him, leaving just this story still unfinished.

When the keeper came back, one half of his face suddenly fell slack. I had never liked that face. In my opinion a churchgoer should not have that kind of face.

"My God."

"My God. The old Chinese man has risen from the dead."

"You do know," the keeper showed admirable self-control, "don't you, that it was only a joke?"

"It was a good story, but a very poor joke." I stopped walking. "Let me tell you the story again. One day you saw an old Chinese man walk into the zoo. You stepped out for a smoke. When you returned the crocodile was gone and just the old man was standing inside the enclosure. That day is today." I raised a leg and slapped at my trousers. They were coated with the powdered remains of Third Master.

"Please stop, old man." The few strands of hair left on the keeper's head seemed to want to float free. "That's quite enough. Let me remind you not to take advantage of April Fool's Day. There is nothing to be gained from it."

"And let me remind you, today is Easter Sunday."

"That was yesterday. Today is April First. This year the day after Easter happens to be April Fool's Day. Please don't pretend you don't know. You understand quite well that you can pull any sort of prank today. But this is going too far. It's not allowable. Legally speaking it's animal cruelty, destruction of cultural heritage. And there's money involved, money!" The keeper's two small fists seemed about to pound his lower belly. "Wait here. Please don't go."

His leather shoes scuffed the ground all the way back to his office.

I am waiting, of course. I am waiting inside a story as though waiting in a cemetery. While alive the graveyard gave me a certain fullness. It gave me more than I could possibly obtain on my own. For this I have to thank the light that you will only ever find in England, a light that seems able to push back time three hundred years. All these things that do not change—the sea, the church, the cemetery—now I am like them. I stopped speaking to other people many years ago. I don't even keep a dog. My only acquaintances here are the bartender at the pub, the butcher, and the baker. I recall the life I once had, when I would rise early to buy a loaf of freshly baked bread, then turn into the butcher's where the owner would hand me a packet of minced meat, exactly a half pound, never a need to weigh it. In the evening I would go to the King's Head for a glass of Scotch, neat. My worries are all behind me, except for the sense of autumn's chill coming on, the thread of cold air stealing in through the wide crimson gate, and the leaves hanging golden on the trees. I miss them, but don't know where they've gone. The more I think of them, the sadder I become, and remember vaguely a large courtyard where the shadows swayed beneath the trees, and something dropped onto the roof ridge. I could not see clearly through the papered window, and just as I made up my mind to run out for a look, Mother's shout stopped me: That's a walnut dropping down from Third Uncle's—you are not allowed to pick it up. That same afternoon, or perhaps it was late that night, more sounds up on the roof . . . .

Not until the police car approached, its siren wailing so loud it rattled the windows, did I realize I could not let them see that the crocodile enclosure held nothing more than a joke.

So the story must be retold.

I climbed out of Third Master's pen and clambered up the other fence. There I saw the heap of crocodiles, the young ones, their mouths gaping open at the sky like scissor blades. I sighed. There is no greater error than to forget that time is never on your side. As I struggled to work my hips over the fence, I heard the sound of teeth grinding.

It was my mother, on her deathbed, biting into a pomegranate. Her lifelong wish had been to eat fresh pomegranate before she died. I had my own wish—to fetch her here to this cemetery, to look after her, to wash her headstone every day. If someone passed by, I too could say that I was tending to my mother. Many times I thought I would discuss this with the church. She would not take up much space. She was in a box, not a coffin.

The last thing I saw was the badge on the hat of the British policeman. It looked exactly like the badge on a China Airlines pilot's cap. No one stopped me. They had to let the story end.

Translated by Harriet Evans and John A. Crespi

Duo Duo was selected as the 2010 laureate of the Neustadt International Prize for Literature, the only international literary prize from the United States for which poets, playwrights, and novelists are given equal consideration. The Neustadt is widely considered to be the most prestigious international prize, after the Nobel Prize for Literature, and is often referred to as the "American Nobel" because of its record of twenty-seven laureates, candidates, or jurors who in the past thirty-nine years have been awarded Nobels following their involvement with the Neustadt. Duo Duo is the twenty-first Neustadt laureate and the first Chinese author to win the prize.

John A. Crespi is the Henry R. Luce Associate Professor of Chinese at Colgate University in Hamilton, New York. He is the author of *Voices in Revolution: Poetry and the Auditory Imagination in Modern China* (University of Hawai'i Press, 2009). His translations of Chinese fiction, prose, and poetry have appeared in a variety of anthologies and literary journals.